LOVE
in the
END
ZONE

CARINA ROSE

LOVE
in the
END
ZONE

TABLE OF CONTENTS

TABLE OF CONTENTS

1

Reese

I PACED THE FLOOR IN the owner's suite, waiting for the game to resume. With only two minutes left, which if played right could feel like twenty, my nerves were frayed.

"Reese, do you want a glass of wine?" My best friend, Alexa, stood at the small bar pouring herself a glass. She wasn't a lover of football as much as she was a lover of football players. I, on the other hand, wanted nothing to do with the latter. What's the saying, don't hate the player, hate the game? Well, I loved the game, getting personal with a player… not so much.

Did I love the team? Yes. It was difficult not to since my granddad, Charles Reese, owned the Virginia Thunder. I knew more stats and rules than the men standing on the field in black-and-white striped shirts did... especially today. I'd never seen so many ridiculous yellow flags hit the turf in one quarter. Then again, God forbid DC Rockets' *golden boy* didn't get into the playoffs. My blood boiled just thinking about Trent Archer.

"No, thank you," I said, snagging another cookie off of the tray, making her laugh. "What?"

"Nothing." Alexa lifted her wineglass in salute before taking a sip.

When I looked at the TV screen in the corner, I saw Trent talking to his coach on the sideline.

Damn, he was gorgeous. The way his sweat-darkened hair hung wispily on his forehead, his defined, scruff-covered jawline, made women and some men swoon. The man had looks that rivaled those of a model. No, actually his were better. Models tended to be pretty, and Trent was anything but pretty. He had an edge to him that made heart rates accelerate... and not just on the field. There had been enough pictures of him with gorgeous women circulating the internet to prove that statement correct.

There were also the many magazines that featured his... well... features. Sexiest athlete, prettiest eyes, and my favorite, best butt. Of course they weren't all in the same publication, and I was sure there were more than just those, but that was the gist of it.

I continued to peruse the six-foot four, two hundred five pounds of pure male as he slid his helmet on and jogged to the Thunder's forty-five-yard line, signaling the end of the fourth quarter's two-minute warning.

Alexa leaned toward me and whispered into my ear. "Remind me why we hate him again? Because I'm thinking that man knows his way around a woman. Look how big his hands are. And wouldn't it be fun—"

"Because he's a jerk," was my reply, cutting her off. I knew what ran around in her head. Yes, I was sure Trent's bedroom skills were above par. They had to be, considering the company he kept. And yes, if circumstances were different, sure, but they weren't different. They were anything but. He was the rival. The enemy. The thorn in my side. The one who sadly got away.

She laughed at my answer, and I shrugged because it was the truth. Growing up, I spent a lot of time with my granddad, and I knew how the business worked. I was so well-versed in the sport that if Granddad would have had his way, I would be sitting in the war room on draft day rather than behind the scenes in my house.

Deciding to try and explain it, I said, "A few years ago, Trent Archer went undrafted. Not because he wasn't an amazing player, but because he got injured during the summer before his senior year. It wasn't anything he couldn't recover from, but he didn't bother to red shirt to avoid ineligibility. Instead, he finished his senior year online, graduated on time, and without any professional prospects. Most thought he had left the sport. Then when the scouting combines started, my granddad had invited him to the Thunder's facility. Other teams heard about it and since my granddad has a stellar reputation, they did the same. His first stop was Nebraska, then Michigan and Indiana. It wasn't until he came to Virginia that things started to get serious.

"Both teams in the area, the DC Rockets and the Virginia Thunder needed a quarterback. Trent knew that and played the game, no pun intended, to get the most lucrative deal." I didn't blame him, who wouldn't want to make the most they could. It was the way he went about it that irked me. "Granddad thought he was a lock and according to Trent's agent, he was… until he wasn't."

Just thinking about that time made my annoyance grow. Granddad's team had been in a slump. They lacked a leader. One who could advance them… one who could sell tickets and fill the seats. My granddad was counting on Trent. I glanced out the glass window to see the majority of the stadium filled with Rockets fans. *At least it was full, I suppose.* I let out a huff before continuing. "Then at the eleventh hour, he signed with the rival DC team."

Alexa's brows drew together. "Ugh. Why?"

"Who knows? Trent's reasoning to the media was… and I quote, 'DC's offer was the right fit' end quote. My guess is he wanted to start right away and with DC's starter coming off an injury, Trent would. With the Thunder, he would have been backup for a year until Donnelly retired. Which I understood. Plus, DC had more money to throw at him than my granddad did. Of course if Granddad hadn't told our GM to invite Trent to training camp, which the media loved, who knows what would have happened. In my opinion nothing. I know for a fact that DC's ticket sales skyrocketed because of the hype. All because of Granddad."

"Wow, he *is* a jerk."

"I'd say. He also did one of my sorority sisters wrong."

"Wait, he went to Sutton?"

"Yes."

"What happened?"

I'll never forget that day. "Our sorority was the 'sister' house to Trent's fraternity. Their fraternity sponsored a silent auction to benefit a charity. The prize was a date to the spring formal with one of the prominent alumni who came out of the fraternity. Tracy Martin, a shy biology major, won. Her choices were a med student, a guy who invented a travel app and started a tech company straight after graduation, or Trent Archer." Alexa looked at me and sighed. "Yup, she picked Trent."

"Was he horrible on their date?"

"Couldn't say because he never showed up. Claimed he had an emergency."

"Ugh."

"Right. Anyway, long story short, Tracy was devastated because it was a big deal on campus. Rather than the school's paper highlighting the event, it highlighted Tracy getting stood up. It was a major debacle. Except for classes, she didn't leave the house for days. The following week a picture of Trent on a beach in California surfaced. It had been taken the same day he should have been with Tracy. I've never immediately disliked a person I didn't know so quickly."

The more I thought about that day combined with everything else, the more annoyed I got. I brought my attention to my granddad who stared at the field with hope in his eyes. Despite knowing the team wouldn't make the playoffs, beating the rivals would be a great way to end the season. He must have sensed my stare because he turned around and smiled. I gave him one in return and a thumbs-up.

Turning to Alexa, I told her I'd be back, grabbed my VIP pass that got me anywhere in the stadium — well, aside from locker rooms, but that was fine with me — slid on my Thunder cap, and headed into the stands. The grooved metal steps were charged with the fans' energy, causing them to vibrate beneath my sneaks. Seeing more Virginia fans made me happy, but sad at the same time.

All of what happened created a domino effect. Without filling the seats and having a losing season, the money wasn't rolling in. *Can't spend what you don't have,* my granddad said to me four years ago when I asked him if he could counter the Rockets' offer.

I understood that too. Regardless of loving the sport and my granddad, I didn't join the family business full on. Instead, I spent my final college years in Europe, graduated magna cum laude with an economics degree, and currently worked at SUGARCOAT, THIS! cookie bakery with Alexa, who owned it with her mother. My sister, Kenzie, and her husband, David, worked in the Thunder's front office. Trust me, they were better suited for those positions. Me, I could be a bit of a hothead and was a much better fit behind the scenes.

During the summer and fall after my junior year in high school, I interned at my granddad's office to get early college credits. I'd sit in meetings and listen to them go on and on about marketing, profit margins, the need for salary caps. They also discussed stats, which I happened to love. Everyone thought I'd be joining the executive team, yet much to their surprise but not my granddad's, I didn't. That didn't mean I wasn't around on draft days or to consult with the senior staff.

It also didn't mean I wasn't a wizard when it came to bizarre information. Sue me, but for some reason that stuff always fascinated me. For instance, Austin Stars are 0–8 against teams with quarterbacks with an E in their first name. Also, the Rockets are 5–0 in the red zone against teams who have a defensive player named Smith while playing on the road. And one more for good measure, the Thunder have more third down conversions while playing against teams that have an animal for a mascot.

I could go on and on, but right now, I had something that needed to be done. Weaving my way through the concession stand lines, I finally came to the gate I wanted. A security guard in a bright yellow jacket stopped me at the top of the stairs before I lifted my badge. He smiled and waved me by. That was another thing. Thanks to keeping a low profile, few people knew who I was. I rarely attended team events, and when I did, I was sure not to be at the forefront. Unless I was promoting the bakery, I did my best to stay away from the media.

The smell of beer, pretzels, and hot dogs brought back a slew of happy memories from when I went to games as a little girl. Remembering the joy on Granddad's face as he explained the rules to his young granddaughters made me happy. This stadium, despite its size, was part of home to me. Call it nostalgia or the fact that I feasted on the energy oozing from the stands, it made me feel alive.

I took the ribbed steps down to the lower level and stood at the railing, bringing myself just left of the goalpost. My ears hummed with the roar of the crowd. The announcer's voice boomed, as the Rockets' fans chanted, *Archer, Archer, Archer.* Trent hiked the ball, handed it off to his running back, and thankfully, our defense stopped him on the twenty-two yard line. A collective moan filled the stadium.

Regardless of knowing there was a five point score difference, I glanced at the scoreboard at the opposite end of the field. That last play took barely any time, and the clock was still running. I let out a long breath, and took a minute to look over at our sideline, hoping our coach would call a time-out, but before he could, Trent went into a no-huddle, hurry-up offense and the next play was off. This time, he threw the ball to his favorite receiver, who went out of bounds at the eleven yard line, stopping the clock with fifteen seconds left.

My heart thumped against my ribs. I knew despite of the game's outcome, the Thunder's seasons was over, but a loss would send the Rockets straight to the post-season. For a moment, I didn't know which was worse—that we weren't going or that they were. Deep down, I knew the Rockets would make it, but hoped it wasn't because they beat us. Bad enough what happened with Trent and my granddad, but the rivalry between the Rockets and Thunder had been going on for decades. I supposed that was what happened when two teams' stadiums were a mere twenty miles apart. We just seemed to be in a slump lately when playing them.

A whistle sounded, my hands wrapped around the painted blue railing, and I stared at Trent. Through the slit in his facemask, I saw his eyes shift from his tight end on his right to the wide receiver on his left. The running back behind him took a step back. I watched as Trent lifted his foot two times as a signal.

He's going to run. I wanted to scream those four words to our defense, but I knew even if I did, they wouldn't hear me, thanks to the tens of thousands of fan's voices and foot stomping wracking the stadium. Our left tackle stepped to the right, and I leaned forward as the ball was hiked.

Trent faked a hand-off and, just like I suspected, he tucked the ball into the number two on his jersey, and ran into the end zone untouched. Defeat hit me straight in my sternum. Poor Granddad.

While the crowd erupted, the refs threw their hands in the air, signaling a touchdown, and I couldn't take my eyes off the field. Annoyance rushed through me that no one in our coach's booth, on the sideline, or on the field read that play correctly. I shook my head. Then that cocky, number-two-wearing baller spiked the pigskin, sending it into the air like a rocket... how fitting.

Naturally, the DC fans around me were high-fiving and chanting, *playoffs* over and over again.

Ignoring the splatters of beer flying in the air, I crossed my arms over my logo-covered chest and stared at the ensuing celebration. At that moment, Trent took off his helmet, seemed to look directly at me, then smiled. No, he didn't just smile, he puckered his lips in a mock kiss right before winking. Jerk! Everything that happened came rushing back… the team, Tracy's devastation, and his egotistical gesture. So, I did what any respectable Thunder fan would do. I lifted my right hand, extended my middle finger, and flipped him off.

I told you I could be a bit of a hothead.

2

Trent

"**P**LAYOFFS BOUND!" MY CENTER YELLED as he thrust his fist into the air. I smiled at him right before taking off my helmet. As soon as it slipped off, the sound of jubilant fans amplified, despite not being in our home stadium. The thing was, we were close enough in proximity and there were more Rockets jerseys than Thunder ones in the crowd.

When I looked up, a gorgeous blonde stared at me. Our eyes connected, and the seventy thousand screaming fans seemed to vanish. It was as though we were in a tunnel, just a pretty girl wearing the home team's colors and me. Her eyes narrowed into a glare. I almost turned around to see what or who she was tossing darts at. Rather than do that, I turned on the charm and blew her a kiss right before I winked—a move I've perfected and most women liked. Much to my surprise, she lifted her hand and flipped me off, causing my mouth to gape. I've had adverse reactions from opposing fans before, but generally they had a beer gut and facial hair. The female population tended to like me. Well, all but this one.

Knowing reporters would be waiting for an interview, I turned and headed toward the sideline. "Who was that?" Jackson, our tight end and my closest friend, chuckled. "Don't tell me there's someone in the DC Metro area who hasn't fallen for the charms of *the* Trent Archer?"

I shoved him and laughed. "Dude, whatever. We're going to the playoffs!"

"Damn straight we are! Woo Hoo!" Jackson jogged off. I couldn't help but look over my shoulder to see if the mystery woman had returned—she hadn't. I hustled past a couple of my teammates being interviewed, smacking them on the shoulder pads as I jogged by. It was great to see them all so happy.

A reporter stopped me. I didn't recognize her, but she had credentials hanging around her neck. "Trent, Veronica Tate, from the *Chronicle,* do you have a minute?" she asked, holding out her mic.

This was what players thrived on. Celebrating. Talking up the team and our season. Not giving some chick in the stands who was bitter about a loss any attention. Granted, I understood the feeling. To feel so passionate about something that you spout off to the first person you come across. No one liked to lose. Still, her reaction irked me.

One of my teammates ran by and slammed a divisional championship cap on my head. I chuckled and brought my attention to the reporter. "Sorry about that, Veronica. Of course, go ahead."

"Thank you. First, congratulations on your win."

I nodded. "Thank you so much. The team worked really hard, and I'm just happy it all paid off. The Thunder is a tough organization. They had us on the ropes today."

"Yes, well, I'm going to jump right in and ask the question everyone is clamoring to know."

I bent at the waist to bring my ear closer to her. I didn't want to miss what she wanted to ask. Although, questions and answers to the obvious were already filtering in my head.

"Was the play to take it yourself designed that way?" – No.

"What do you plan on fixing, moving on to the playoffs?" – The team will go over today's film and study. I'll get back to you on that one.

"You have the Austin Stars next. Do you think the Rockets' defensive line can handle Austin's explosive offense?" – That's an easy one, yes. Of course, after that I'd wink. Didn't want to appear too arrogant.

"Do you think you'll be the league's MVP?" — *There are a lot of skilled players in the league. I'd be honored, but that isn't my goal. Winning it all for DC is.*

Veronica nodded to her cameraperson, who took a step closer. "What did you do to the woman in the stands to provoke such a... well... greeting?"

I straightened and stared at Veronica. How did she see the woman in the stands? And that was her question? I shifted my focus to the camera and smirked. "Well, I guess that was her way of telling me I was number one in her book."

The man behind the lens chuckled. Veronica gave me a weak grin. "So not an ex?" *Was she writing a sports' article or a gossip column?* When I didn't answer, Veronica wrapped up what she called an interview. "Good luck next week."

"Thanks," I said dryly and did my best to hide my annoyance before moving on to a couple more interviews about the game and not an opinionated blonde.

Jackson and I sat in my living room relaxing with beer and watching the Sunday night game between the Austin Stars and the Nebraska Lightning. The outcome didn't matter, since Nebraska was in a rebuilding year. They had a great organization, and they were in the running, but I got a better offer.

"Stars look good," Jackson said, taking a pull from the longneck bottle.

"They do." I observed their defensive lineman barely missing a sack.

"Look out for him."

We watched the first half, taking notes and coming up with a few plays we would run by the coach on Tuesday since we had tomorrow off.

The whistle signaling halftime blew and a commercial came on. I pushed off the leather chair and stood. "Want another beer?"

Jackson lifted his bottle, drained it, and nodded. "Sure, thanks." The doorbell rang. "That must be the pizza, I'll grab it."

"Okay, I'll get our beer."

With our dinner and drinks, we plopped onto the sofa just as my face popped up on the screen.

"There's our pretty boy," Jackson crooned, chuckling around a piece of pepperoni.

Ignoring him, I went to take a bite of my slice when an image appeared. No, not really an image, a meme. A meme of the girl flipping me off, with the Thunder's logo over her finger on one side, and me on the other. Despite her crassness, she looked gorgeous. I, on the other hand, looked dumbfounded. Wide eyes, mouth in the shape of an O, and the caption, "Are you talking to me?" scrawled across my chest.

Jackson's laugh had me scowling. "Oh my God.

This is too good." Then he paused. "Wait… what did they just say her name was?"

"I don't know, jackass, you were too busy laughing." I grabbed the remote off the coffee table, and rewound the broadcast.

"Thunder's owner, Charles Reese's granddaughter and namesake, Reese Parker, seemed to have a message for America's favorite quarterback."

Everything started to sound like a mess of blurred words. "Granddaughter?" I whispered. That wasn't Reese's granddaughter. I met her. She was a brunette, worked in the front office with her husband.

"Looks like you pissed off a part of his family," Jackson offered as an explanation. "But wow is she gorgeous. And practically football royalty. Great job."

Jackson knew I had almost signed with the Thunder. He also knew how I struggled with the decision that was made for me. That withstanding, obscene gestures caught on camera weren't my thing. Still staring at the screen, I shook my head and used my pizza slice as a pointer to the image in front of us. "Dude, I'm a meme. This is the last thing I need before playoffs. Do you know what this means? My social media is going to be blowing up."

"Don't let it distract you or coach will flip out."

Flip out? He was going to lose it. One thing Coach Mark prided himself on was his players keeping their noses clean. Despite any fines a league could impose for behavior unbecoming, he had his own set of rules. None of this was my fault, but still, he might not see it that way. "You're right. I need to put a stop to it."

Jackson nodded and took another bite out of the slice in his hand. After swallowing, he asked, "How do you plan on doing that? Looks like the media loves her."

When I glanced at the television, images of Reese at the local children's hospital, volunteering at a school in the city, and then serving dinner at one of the shelters on Thanksgiving flitted across the screen. In each image she had a tray of cookies in her hand.

"Yeah, and she loves sweets."

"Are you not listening?"

"To what? I'm watching this just like you."

He bobbed his head up and down. "Then you know she works at a cookie bakery." *Well, that made sense.* Weird that she didn't work for her grandfather, especially being so *passionate* about the game. "So, now what?" he asked, knowing me well enough to realize a plan was formulating in my mind.

"Looks like it's time to satisfy my sweet tooth."

"What are you going to do? Order cookies in hopes to get in her good graces?"

"No, I'm going to ask her out on a date."

Beer flew out of Jackson's mouth and sprayed my coffee table. He leaned forward and wiped it up with his napkin before turning toward me and grinning. My tight end and best friend knew that when I put my mind to something, I didn't let it falter. Right now, all that mattered was the post-season and bringing the championship trophy to DC. A meme of a ticked-off fan, regardless of her relation to the rival team, would not distract me.

"Pardon me for pointing out the obvious, but I don't think she likes you."

He was right. Except Reese Parker didn't know me. But after tomorrow, I'd make sure that wasn't the case.

3

Reese

EACH TIME I CLOSED MY eyes, Trent Archer's smug face would pop up and invade my thoughts. I needed to stop letting him get under my skin. Especially since he had no clue who I was. Still, I couldn't purge him from my mind. The arrogance of that wink infuriated me. And if I were being a bit honest, it was sexy as hell. Too bad I despised him.

After the game, I went home and warmed up last night's Thai takeout, plopped down on my sofa, and flicked on the television to watch the late game. Despite being out of the postseason, I wanted to see who would be taking on the Rockets. Except it was halftime, and an image of me in the stands decked out in my favorite Thunder quarter-zip and cap appeared in a square next to the host's head, then it switched to a side-by-side of me and Trent.

We're a meme?

Then I looked at Trent's face. Since I had left after *saluting* him, I never saw his reaction. A deep laugh rumbled out of me when I saw his shocked expression. Maybe I should be upset that *my* face was front and center, but seeing his wide eyes and gaped mouth made my earlier annoyance dissipate.

Just as I slid some noodles into my mouth, my phone rang. Kenzie's name illuminated my screen. *Well, better get this over with.* I set my bowl down, wiped my hands, and tapped the green icon connecting the call.

"Hi, Kenz," I perkily greeted, knowing she'd be upset with me.

"Seriously, Reese? You flipped off Trent Archer?"

"Yeah, well, he's a jerk. He blew me a kiss and winked! What was I supposed to do? Wink back?"

She sighed. Kenzie and I were closer than most sisters. Our mom passed away shortly after I was born and since our dad couldn't take it, he left his two daughters. But not before demanding a financial payment from our grandfather since everything in our mother's will went to Kenzie and me. Knowing what a sleaze-bag our father was, Granddad reluctantly paid him a generous sum, so he would stay out of our lives. Mission accomplished because the man was only after our mother's money and never with her for love.

Thankfully after that, our maternal grandparents took us in and raised us. Because of *that*, it strengthened our bond as sisters, yet we couldn't be more different.

"Well, our PR department is trying to get a handle on things. You can't just go around and give the finger to people, no matter how obnoxious they are. Grandpa—"

"Grandpa, what?" I asked, finally letting the pit in my stomach plummet. The last thing I wanted to do was upset him. It was bad enough our season ended at the hand of the Rockets. Rubbing salt into that wound, wasn't my intention.

"He told me to let it go. You have a right to express yourself."

I smiled, crisscrossed my legs, and relaxed into my sofa. "He's right, you know."

"You're just his favorite." *True.* "Will you please do me a favor and try not to do anything else? We don't need any bad press heading into the off-season."

"Of course. I'll be on my best behavior." If she were in front of me, rather than on the phone, I would have given her a mock salute.

"Thank you." Kenzie's exhale sounded loud and clear. "Trent's contract is up this season."

"Yes, I know that, but it's not like he's not going

to sign with the Rockets. We need to move on from Archer. Davis from Rochester and Park from Boulder look fantastic. They'll definitely go first or second round. Did you know Davis threw for a school high of almost four thousand passing yards this season… threw thirty touchdowns and rushed for six? He has over a seventy percent completion percentage. Not to mention, he's only twenty-two. In addition to Davis and Park, there's McCarthy from Omaha. He threw for over three thousand yards and has a completion percentage over sixty. Then there's—"

"I understand there are great players. What I don't understand is why you prefer to work in a bakery. You're born to work with us. No one knows stats like you do."

"Because cookies don't piss me off. And I do work there when needed."

She let out a laugh. "Fine, and your statistical prowess is appreciated. Draft day is right around the corner."

"Yes, I know. I'll be there like I am every year."

Kenzie knew I collaborated with our grandfather and executive team before the draft. Heck, she knew I worked behind the scenes all the time and not only around draft day. Just because I didn't devote all of my time to being at the office, didn't mean I was less involved. On some level, I was more involved than those who had a nameplate on their door.

"Okay. I need to get going. Oh, and thank you for taking care of Bubba while we're away. I'll drop him off in the morning."

"Yes, I'm looking forward to spending time with my nephew."

She laughed. "Try to stay out of trouble. I love you, Reese."

"Love you too, Kenz."

The call ended; I tossed my phone onto the coffee table and resumed eating my dinner. Thoughts of Trent needed to be pushed to the back of my brain. We needed to focus on next season. There were a few other college prospects and thanks to an eight and ten season, we should be able to get a good drafting position. But despite the amazing collegiate numbers in this upcoming draft class, we needed experience. Tomorrow I'd call Granddad and discuss everything. For now, all I wanted to do was finish my dinner, go to bed, and think about anything but football... and a gorgeous quarterback.

Thanks to my unwanted publicity, Sugarcoat This! was mobbed the following day. Alexa and her mother, Erica, had a difficult time keeping up. At one point, I tried to apologize, but Erica waved me off, reminding me that sales meant money. Thankfully, there were only a couple reporters who popped in to ask questions. Most respected my granddad enough not to bother me, but that didn't mean they weren't all itching for a story... and what better one than why America's favorite quarterback received a rude hand gesture.

All day a steady stream of customers filled the small store. It wasn't until we finally had a lull, that I took a break. Alexa had taken hers earlier since she needed to run to the bank. My feet were killing me, my hair was falling out of my ponytail, and I was sure I looked ragged.

"I'm going to head to the back and sit for a few minutes." I moved from behind the counter, and the bell above the door chimed. It was as though I could sense him. Of course, Alexa and Erica's collective gasp didn't help matters. When I pivoted, my blue eyes locked onto Trent's magnetic green ones. I didn't even know if that was the correct way to describe them. They were lush and full with ambition... utterly breathtaking.

What am I doing? The last thing I should be thinking about are his eyes. Despite how captivating they are.

He strode in like he'd been to the bakery a million times before. Trent glanced at Alexa and her mother who were just staring at him. "Good afternoon, ladies."

Alexa's face bloomed with a pink hue. Erica smiled and nudged her daughter, who choked out a hello before her mom disappeared through the kitchen door behind her. It was as though everything happened in slow motion.

Breaking the lovefest going on, I headed toward him, and popped my hands on my hips. "What are you doing here?"

With confident strides, Trent made his way to me, smiling and nodding at a couple customers in the process. His long legs encased in dark denim and his black shirt underneath a black leather biker jacket made him look like a movie star. He ran his hand through his hair, and his lips tipped up into a devilish smirk that made my insides flutter. *Has to be nerves.*

"I'm here to see you, of course."

"Perfect timing. Reese was just going on her break," Alexa offered, looking a bit star-struck. "Can I get you coffee or a cookie? I'm Alexa, by the way. The best friend."

He traded his smirk for a model-worthy smile, and I swore I saw the traitor behind the counter steady herself. "Pleasure to meet you, I'm Trent, but you probably already know that." Alexa nodded slowly. "And thank you, I'd love a coffee. One sugar and two creams, please. And why don't you pick the cookie. Whatever your favorite is. Actually, box up a couple dozen. I'll take them to the guys tomorrow."

In less than a minute, Alexa brought over his coffee and a plate with a blue-frosted sugar cookie on it and set them on a small round table. "Let's sit," Trent said to me, pulling out a chair.

My so-called friend waved at me behind his

back urging me to comply with his request. Not wanting to make a scene, I sat.

"What can I do for you?"

"Well, first off, I'd like to introduce myself."

What game was he playing? "I know who you are, and you clearly know who I am, so let's cut to the chase."

"Okay. Well, Miss Parker... it is miss, right?" I nodded, he smirked, and I crossed my legs beneath the table. "It appears you have a poor opinion of me, and I'd like to rectify that. Especially since you don't have a valid reason to. Well, except for the *loss* yesterday."

My eyes automatically narrowed. "Are you trying to win me over or something? If that's the case, you're failing miserably."

Trent took a sip of his coffee and licked his lips. "Sorry. Let's start over." He extended his hand. "I'm Trent Archer, and I'd like to be friends."

A snort-laugh flew out of my mouth. "No, but thank you."

"Your grandfather said you wouldn't be so forgiving. Even he understands I was just doing my job."

"My granddad? You went to see my granddad? Why? When? Why?"

Trent chuckled and took a bite of his cookie. I sat there, getting more annoyed by the second. "Wow, this is delicious," he said through chews.

After swallowing, he lifted the cookie. "Are you sure you don't want some?" When I remained silent he smirked. "Here's the deal, I have profound respect for Mr. Reese, and when I found out that you were his granddaughter, I knew I had to say something to him. The last thing I'd want is for him to think poorly of me. So, I went to his office to have a chat. Oh, your sister says hi."

All I could do was blink. Did I fall asleep on my break? Was I hallucinating? When I remained silent, he added, "Have dinner with me tonight."

Just as I was about to say no, my phone rang. Thank God, saved by the bell. When I saw it was my granddad, I let out a breath. "Excuse me," I said before connecting the call. "Hi, Granddad."

"Hey, baby girl. Trent came to see me, and I have a feeling you're going to be his next stop."

I lifted my eyes to meet Trent's, whose were softening by the second. "Yes, you're correct."

"Ahh, he's there. Okay, look. I know you're upset, and your passion is appreciated, but don't burn bridges. I understand your animosity toward the man, but honey, he's a good person." *Tracy Martin doesn't think so,* I wanted to blurt out, but knowing that wouldn't make any sense, I refrained. Turning away from Trent, I cupped my hand over my mouth, and whispered, "Are you asking me to take one for the team?"

My granddad laughed. "Of course not. I'd never do that. All I wanted to do was remind you that what we do is a business. The man made his choice. We're coming up on a new season and made changes to the salary cap. We'll be okay. You know that better than anyone."

I did know that. It still didn't mean I was ready to fall for Trent's charms.

We said our goodbyes and he hung up. "Well, my break is over."

Trent stood. "Dinner tonight?"

"I'm not going to date you."

"Did I say date? I said dinner."

Not understanding the difference, I tried another tactic. "It's been a long day. Plus, don't you leave for Austin tomorrow?"

"Yes, but we both need to eat." He rubbed the back of his neck. "Look, I just want to talk to you, that's it. If not, I suppose I can just hang out here. Or come back every day until you agree."

The man was nothing if not exasperating. Begrudgingly, I relented. "Fine, but it's not a date."

That sexy as sin, leave-your-panties-at-the-door smirk appeared. No doubt the man perfected it with years of practice. We agreed to me making dinner at my house since I liked home field advantage. He said goodbye to Alexa and Erica, signed an autograph and took a selfie with a teenaged boy, then walked out.

Glancing over to a beaming Alexa, I shook my head, wondering what I just got myself into.

4

Trent

REESE IS BEAUTIFUL. THE MORE I thought about the outspoken woman, the more I wanted to get to know her. She intrigued me on a level different from any woman I'd ever met. Maybe it was because my profession didn't matter to her. She'd been around athletes and the sport so much, the last thing she probably wanted was to date a player. Still, I wasn't about to let that deter me.

I pulled up to her house, grabbed the bouquet of white and yellow roses and the bottle of wine I picked up on the way, and got out of the car. Her home was on a quiet street nestled between rows of trees. The classic two-story structure suited her. It was understated and beautiful, much like her.

Giving myself a once-over, I ran my hand through my hair before ringing her doorbell. The sound of barking caught my attention first. Through the wooden door, I could hear her muted voice talking to what I assumed was the dog. She pulled the door open and smiled. The little puffy white pup she held wiggled, looking as though it wanted to jump out of her arms and into mine.

"Hi, come on in." Reese stepped aside and closed the door behind me.

"Cute dog."

"It's not mine. My sister and her husband went on vacation and left Bubba with me."

I couldn't help but laugh. The dog looked more like soft cotton, and its sparkly blue collar didn't seem like an accessory someone named Bubba would wear.

"The dog's name is Bubba?"

Reese nodded and set him down. "Yes. Dave, that's my brother-in-law, conceded to my sister's choice in getting a Bichon, but with the stipulation that he could pick the name." She shrugged and looked at the fluff ball, who was currently smelling my Italian leather loafers. "I think he thought Kenzie would change her mind. She didn't... clearly."

"Clearly," I said, handing Reese the flowers and wine. "These are for you. I wasn't sure what was on the menu, so I brought a rosé."

"Thank you." She walked into her kitchen, put the flowers in a vase she pulled from the cabinet above her refrigerator, and set the wine on the counter.

Meanwhile, I bent down to pick up Bubba. "Aren't you a cutie?" His little tongue decided to bathe my jaw. "I think he likes me."

"He likes everyone," she touted, walking back into the room.

I held the dog in the air so our noses were a couple inches apart. "That's not true is it, Bubba?" The dog repeatedly licked my face. "I didn't think so." Reese shook her head. I chuckled, set Bubba down, and took off my jacket.

"Here, I'll take that." Reese hung it in the foyer closet. My eyes took the opportunity to scan her body. Her light-colored jeans hung loose on her slim frame. When she lifted her arms to hang my jacket, the red sweater she wore rose just enough to expose the top of two dimples on her lower back, which I happened to find ridiculously sexy. I was almost busted when she quickly turned and closed the closet door. "Dinner should be ready shortly. Would you like something to drink?" She rattled off a couple of options before I settled on a beer.

"I like your house." Taking a moment, I took in the cottage style décor, including a stone fireplace with built-in shelves on either side. The charcoal gray wood flooring contrasting to the white walls was strikingly beautiful... much like the owner.

A beaming smile grew across her face. "Thank

you." She walked into the main room with my beer and a glass of wine in her hand. "Here you go."

We sat down and a picture on the side table caught my eye. Reese wore a black graduation gown with a red honor stoles around her neck along with another one with Greek letters. Her grandfather stood next to her in front of a familiar building. "You went to Sutton?" She nodded. "How could we have gone to the same university, without me knowing that?"

"Because you were gone when I got there. I was a freshman your senior year." That would make Reese around twenty-three or twenty-four. Although, I didn't plan on confirming that assumption.

"And your sorority?"

"Gamma Pi Delta."

"That was my frat's sister sorority."

"I know." Something in her snippy tone had me wondering if maybe we had met before, but there was no way I wouldn't have remembered. The timer on her oven beeped; Bubba sprang up and followed her into the kitchen, preventing me from asking why she sounded ticked off about that.

Opting to abandon the previous conversation, I stood and walked toward her. "Everything smells great." Reese pulled a casserole dish from the oven and set it on a hot plate in the center of the table. I hadn't noticed the salad and rolls already there.

"Thank you. I hope you like it."

We sat down and she plated our dinners. I didn't know when the last time a woman, other than my mother or my housekeeper, cooked for me. Reese wasn't only stunning, she was a great cook. We ate in silence, and before long, my plate was empty. When I looked up, she was staring at me.

"Sorry, I was hungry and well, this is the best thing I've eaten in a long time. You're a very good cook."

"Thank you. I love cooking. Kenzie and I learned at an early age." She looked as though she wanted to give me insight to why that was, but instead she motioned toward the casserole. "Please help yourself to more."

She didn't need to tell me twice. Once my plate was filled with my second round of chicken, rice, and broccoli, I decided to ask the question that has been bothering me. "Why do you dislike me so much?"

Reese placed her fork down and dabbed her lips with her napkin. "I don't dislike you…" I cocked a brow. Her lips quirked up in the corners before she added, "Much."

"So, you generally give people you like the finger?"

"Not usually, no."

"What can I do to make you change your mind

about me? Because I can't stop thinking about you. I think you should give me a shot."

"A shot at what?"

"Dating you—" Before I even finished what I wanted to say, she shook her head, sending her blonde hair swaying on her shoulders.

"Hear me out. I think we'd be good together. If nothing else, we can be friends."

"You don't even know me. How could you think that?"

"I know you love your family, you understand football, and you have a soft spot for animals. I also know you protect those you care about." I went on to say, "I too love my family, also have football running through my veins, and like animals. See… match made in heaven."

"Those are hardly reasons to date."

She got up and carried her almost empty plate to the sink and turned the water on. I followed, stood behind her, bringing my chest a breath away from her back. Reese's floral perfume tickled my senses. I could feel every part of my body begin to react to her. If I wasn't careful, she was going to think I was only after one thing.

Reese turned off the faucet, then looked over her shoulder and tilted her head back. Her lips were mere inches away from mine. What would she do if I leaned forward and kissed her? It wouldn't take much, just a slight dip of my head.

Then again, if blowing her a kiss and winking earned me her middle finger, would our lips touching force her to punch me? Not wanting to risk it, I stepped back.

Reese's chest rose and fell with a few deep breaths, her cheeks pinkened, and if I didn't know better, I'd say she was just as affected by our close proximity as I had been. Taking a chance, I confessed. "You have no idea how badly I want to kiss you."

"I'm not sure that's such a great idea."

"Or it could be the best idea. Actually, could be the best kiss you've ever had."

She failed at suppressing a grin. "You're awfully confident."

"It's my nature."

I should be happy that she didn't flat-out decline, and, not wanting to seem like a prick, I nodded and went to the table to get my plate. We silently worked in tandem cleaning the dinner dishes as though we'd done it a million times together, and when we were done, I thought she'd ask me to leave. Instead, she opened a cabinet and pulled out a pink box that I recognized from the bakery.

She put a few cookies on a small dish. "Would you like some coffee?"

"No, thank you."

Reese brewed herself a cup and carried it along

with the sweets into the family room. She sat on the couch, but I couldn't stop myself from walking to the built-ins. Books, pictures, and a few awards adorned the shelves. Most of the framed images were of her and her grandfather, her sister, and a woman holding a baby.

"That's my mother." I turned and strode to where she was sitting and made myself comfortable on the opposite end of the sofa. "She passed away shortly after I was born."

"I'm sorry. I understand how important family is."

"Thank you. Yes, they are. You were right, I am very protective of those I care about. It probably stems from my childhood. My grandparents stepped in and gave us a wonderful life." She sipped her coffee and abruptly changed the subject. "Congratulations on the playoffs."

I couldn't help but laugh. "How hard was that to say? Your face looks like you just bit into a dill pickle."

"First, I happen to love dill pickles, and second, just a little." She gave me a tight grin. "The Rockets are a good team. You just need to watch your tells."

"My tells?"

"Yes, you have certain quirks. If I had a headset and direct line to the defensive coordinator, that final play yesterday would have resulted in a sack and not you running into the end zone."

My head reared back. No way did I give anything away at the line. When Reese gave a silent *whatever* via a nonchalant shrug, my curiosity piqued. "Okay, why don't you enlighten me? What did I do that prompted you to think you knew the play we were going to run?"

"Hmm... I'm not sure I should say anything."

I rested my right ankle on my left knee and stretched my arm on the sofa's back cushion, making myself comfortable. In other words, *I've got all night.*

Reese rolled her eyes. "Fine. I'll tell you." *Okay, maybe she can read my mind.* "When you're going to throw a screen, you tap your center's back twice, when you're going to hand the ball to your running back, you tilt your hip to the left or right depending on which way the defense lines up, and yesterday, you looked at your tight end before shifting your eyes and giving a slight nod to the defensive back who was ready to block your wide receiver." She casually raised one shoulder. "It was a bold move. That's when I knew you were going to take it yourself."

If I hadn't been so shocked, I would have been completely turned on. No, scratch that. Hearing her describe my offensive play had me needing to readjust my pants. That had to be the hottest thing anyone had ever said to me.

"Do you know how sexy you are?"

She laughed and, once again, I wanted to kiss

her. Instead, I picked up a cookie and polished it off, giving my mouth something else to do. Except something told me Reese's lips would be sweeter.

"I'm sexy because I know what play you're going to call?"

I shook my head. "No, you're sexy because you understand the game I live for. Knowing you watch me so intently is what turns me on." Her face took on a rosy hue. "I like this side of you much better than the expressive fan in the stands. But since I don't want to press my luck, I'm going to call it a night."

We both stood, Reese retrieved my jacket, and I slid it on while she picked up Bubba. I palmed my phone and unlocked it. "Can I have your number?" When she paused, I added, "Please?" To my surprise, she rattled off ten digits. After I immediately dialed them and her phone rang, I hung up. "Now you have mine. Will you be watching the game this weekend?"

"Yes, of course."

"Good. I'll be sure to make the necessary offensive adjustments." I stepped onto the porch. "Thanks again for dinner. See ya, Bubba."

She nodded, and the white puffball barked. If it didn't sound ridiculous, I'd say that puppy was smiling. I turned to leave, and she said, "Trent, watch out if Beckett lines up in the Stars' backfield. If he swaps with Sanchez, he's going to blitz. Oh, and the Stars, they are 0-8 against quarterbacks with an E in their first name. So you have that going for you."

Who was this woman? "Anything else?"

"Bailey falls for a hard count. He leads the league in neutral zone infractions and false starts. Free yardage up for grabs."

That one I knew about, but didn't let on that I did. "Noted. Thanks, Reese."

"What are friends for?" The bright smile that lit up her face had me reciprocating with one of my own.

"Friends." I bobbed my head a few times. "I can live with that… for now."

We stared at each other for a long minute until she moved back and closed the door. I had no idea what just happened, except I knew Reese Parker could change my life.

5

Reese

FOR THE PAST FEW DAYS all I could think about was Trent. I mean, how could I not? The man sent me a text thanking me for dinner, then another the following day to tell me he landed in Austin, and of course, one today to remind me to watch the game. As if I'd forget?

At the sound of my doorbell, Bubba started barking. I scooped him up. "It's just Alexa coming over to hang out with us." When I opened the door, she immediately took Bubba from me and started kissing his poofy head. "Hi to you too."

She laughed. "I love when you dog-sit Bubba. You really need to get one of your own."

"How about you get one of *your* own?"

Alexa plopped down and Bubba instantly

curled up on her lap. The infomercial on TV ended and the pre-game show came on. The camera panned the football field where the Rockets and the Stars were both warming up.

"Whoever created football pants was a genius," Alexa said staring at the screen.

I couldn't help but laugh and agree with her. The camera landed on Trent and if anyone looked good in a uniform, it was him. Naturally, he looked good in jeans too. I had a feeling the man would look good wearing a karate uniform and not many people could pull off that look—black belt or not.

"Damn." Alexa whistled. "That man's ass should be illegal."

"Alexa Barton, I can't believe you just said that."

"Why?" she asked, pointing to the television. "Look at it." I couldn't stop my eyes from focusing on how football pants enhanced the perfect slope of his backside. Pulling from that thought, she sighed. "And who the heck is that next to him? Wow."

Not affected in the least, I answered her plainly. "That's Cartwright. He's the tight end."

"He sure is…"

"Okay, enough ogling. I made some margaritas. Would you like one?" She nodded, never taking her eyes off the television.

I headed to the kitchen, poured us each a drink, made a quick batch of nachos, and put everything on a tray including a treat bone for Bubba.

Alexa took a sip of the chartreuse cocktail. "Mmm... I could have helped you."

"It's fine, I wouldn't want to distract you."

She giggled. "So, we've been so busy all week, you never told me how your evening went with Trent."

Alexa was right. Ever since word got out that the woman who flipped off Trent Archer worked at the bakery, there hadn't been a dull moment. Alexa even made cookies in the shape of birds and frosted them in the Thunder's colors of blue and silver. She also cut the wing to look like its middle feather was sticking out a bit. If you didn't know the story behind it, you'd never notice—except most people did. We couldn't keep them on the shelves. Because of that, she spent most of the time in the back kitchen.

I gave her a quick rundown, then found myself admitting, "He said he wanted to kiss me. And between you, me, and Bubba, I was tempted. Then I remembered how he did us wrong, and I don't know... it just didn't feel right. We did agree to be friends though."

Her eyes studied me, and she blinked a few times before shaking her head. "I get it, I do, but Reese, the man is beyond good-looking. I know you feel he screwed over your grandfather and yes, he stood up your friend, but that was in the past. He was young. Plus, you said it yourself that your grandfather seemed to be fine with him."

Everything she said was right. Still, I'd never forget the devastation on Tracy's face and my granddad's. That was two strikes. Was I supposed to take the chance and possibly be number three? I don't think so.

"Did you ask him about Tracy?"

"Pfft, no. Although, he does know I was in his frat's sister sorority."

His voice sounded through the speakers, forcing my head to snap to the broadcast. Trent stood on the sideline talking to a reporter.

"What do you need to do in order to win today?"

"Even I know that's a dumb question," Alexa said, making me giggle.

"Our offense needs to score, and our defense needs to prevent them from doing the same." I snort-laughed and Alexa let out a giggle of her own. Then he looked into the camera. "Other than that, we need to play tough. Oh, and I need to watch how I tilt my hips." Trent winked, and I felt it down to my toes.

"What did that mean?" Alexa asked, and I shrugged while sporting a goofy grin. "Okay, what gives?"

"I told him he does certain things that give

away what play he's going to run. It's not an all the time thing, just occasionally." I went on talking in football lingo and when she just blinked, I shut my mouth.

"You know I love you, right?"

"Of course."

"And I love you working at the bakery, but honey, you belong beside your grandfather full-time. Heck, you belong in the coach's booth. Maybe you should consider taking a more active role."

"You sound like everyone else. And just like I said to them, I will consult and run stats for drafts and trades. Aside from that, I'm happy doing what I'm doing. Granddad also knows, when and if he needs me, I'll be there. Plus, he has Kenzie and Dave." Bubba's head lifted at the mention of his parents before returning to attack the peanut butter shoved into the rubber bone.

"And Trent? Are you going to give him a shot? I mean, I get you agreed to be friends, but he seems to really like you. Do you know how many women would kill to be in your position right now?"

"More power to them."

Alexa popped a chip into her mouth and shook her head. "I love you, but you're clearly in denial."

"Denial about what?"

She pointed to the television. "Him! Trent. I don't believe for one second you're not hot for him."

"You're wrong."

"Am I?"

I shrugged just as our national anthem came on, and we stopped talking to listen. It never failed that my eyes filled at the sound of that song. Then the game started, and for the next couple of hours, we drank tequila-spiked drinks, munched on Tex-Mex food, and no longer talked about the gorgeous quarterback with the best butt on the field. Instead, we watched the Rockets win, sending them to the final game.

Once Alexa had gone home and Bubba was curled into his bed next to mine, I grabbed my phone and sent Trent a text, congratulating him on his win.

See, I can be nice, I thought setting my phone on my nightstand. When the phone dinged a few seconds later, I couldn't help but feel joy.

> **Trent:** *Thank you. Good thing I didn't blow their perfect record against quarterbacks with E in their name.*

I smiled that he remembered my ridiculous stat I shared with him. Rather than reply, I sent a thumbs up emoji, set down my phone, and did my best to get some sleep.

After handing a customer her order, the bell above the door sounded. Alexa gasped and muttered, *good Lord.* The customer at the counter and I turned, and I swore the woman swayed. She even grabbed the counter for support! In walked Trent, Jackson Cartwright, and Troy Davis, the Rockets' backup quarterback. I hadn't formally met the other guys, but Troy was on my radar as a prospect for the Thunder. He was meant to be a starter but with Trent having a fantastic season, it wouldn't be happening unless Trent didn't get re-signed by the Rockets. And unless something catastrophic occurred, there was no way he wouldn't get another deal.

"Holy smokes, they're stunning," Alexa breathed into my ear. "The younger one looks like he could be Michael B. Jordan's understudy."

When I locked eyes with Trent, he smiled. Seeing these guys on the field was one thing but seeing them in street clothes was something on an entirely different level. My libido decided to wake up, thanks to Trent in his once again dark denim jeans, black leather jacket over an equally dark shirt. It didn't help my *situation* that his messy chestnut hair accentuated his green eyes, making them look like jewels. Of course, I'd never admit that to Alexa.

On the other hand, Jackson's jeans were lighter, his worn leather jacket and longer dark hair made him look like a complete bad-boy—a persona the media ate up and women lost their minds over. Apparently, that included my friend who couldn't stop staring at him. He stood about an inch or two shorter than Trent, but still over six-feet tall, then there was Troy. His boy-next-door, movie star look landed him many magazine covers, despite currently sitting on the bench.

Murmurs from the customers sitting at tables enjoying their coffee filled the otherwise quiet air. Thankfully, no one made a big deal about the guys. That being said, the high school hadn't let out yet. If those students were in here, both boys and girls would swarm them.

"Good afternoon, gentlemen. What's your pleasure?" Alexa's singsong voice had me shaking my head. I loved my best friend… and she loved and appreciated the male gender. It was one of the reasons she liked going to football games.

Jackson strolled to the glass case and peered inside before looking up at a blushing Alexa. "What's *your* pleasure? I'm Jackson, this here's Troy, and you know Trent."

"Alexa." Her voice sounded as though she'd just run a marathon.

"Nice to meet you." He looked at me. "Reese, it's good to meet you."

"Likewise. Hi, Troy."

"Hey," he casually replied.

Trent locked eyes with me and chuckled before

glancing into the case. "Is that a bird... with a protruding middle feather?" He looked at me once more and let out a hearty laugh.

Troy leaned in and joined the laughing brigade. "Oh, that's too good. I'll take a dozen," he said to Alexa.

I grabbed a cleaning cloth, walked around the counter, and busied myself wiping off a couple tables. The guys ordered their beverages of choice, and like always, Trent's presence filled the room. I turned and smiled. "Congratulations again on your win. Did you guys just get back?"

"Yes, came here straight from Dulles. We had our team meeting on the plane. Once we were in the car, I suddenly had a craving for something sweet."

"Well then, you came to the right place." His eyes roamed up and down my body, sending what felt like a zing of electricity through my veins.

"Can you sit for a minute?"

"Sure?"

"Did you answer my question with a question?"

"Oh," I laughed at myself. "I can sit for a minute." He pulled out my chair for me. "Thank you."

We stared at each other, neither of us saying anything. For once, I had nothing to say. Well, that wasn't completely true. I wasn't sure how to act.

For so long, he was enemy number one, now we agreed to be friends. Except, all I could do was focus on his lips. Even during the game, when the cameraperson zoomed in on Trent calling a play, my eyes went straight to his mouth.

"If you keep looking at me like that, I'm going to want something in my mouth other than a cookie."

Heat inched its way up my spine and settled beneath my ponytail. "Friends don't say things like that to friends."

"Friends don't look at each other the way you're looking at me."

"Touché, I guess." I could have easily played along and asked how I was looking at him, but I knew. I also knew that hearing him describe it would have had me reaching across the table, grabbing his jacket, and fusing our lips together. *Seriously, Reese, get it together.*

Just then Bubba's high-pitched bark came from the back room. He had his own play area, but probably needed to go outside. Kenzie told me I could leave him at my house, but then he looked at me with those sweet, round, dark eyes, and before I knew it, he was strapped into the doggie seat in my car.

"Is that my pal, Bubba?"

"It is. Can you excuse me please?"

I got up and noticed that Alexa was sitting and

laughing with Troy and Jackson while Erica manned the counter. After I opened the door leading to the small breakroom, a cute face greeted me. "Do you need to go outside, sweet boy?" Bubba's tail spun, leaving a circular indentation in his fur. "I'll take that as a yes." I bent over and lifted him up. As soon as I had him in my arms, he started to squirm, and I knew exactly why.

"Hey, Bubba, remember me?" The dog's small pink tongue hung out of his mouth as he panted with excitement. Trent reached forward and took him.

"Be careful, he needs to pee." I grabbed his leash, attached it to his collar, and Trent finally set him down.

"Well, we wouldn't want any accidents, now would we?" Trent's tone took on a lilt as he addressed my dog-nephew.

"Come on, let's go outside."

The cold air cut straight through my long-sleeved cotton shirt. I muttered how much I detested the winter when suddenly Trent's jacket was around my shoulders. Leather mixed with his manly cologne teased my nose. It took every ounce of self-control not to turn my head and bury my face in the collar.

We walked, leaving footprints in the snow until we came to a tree Bubba seemed to favor. He lifted his leg and did his business.

"Good boy, Bubba. Now let's go back inside and get a treat." The sweet dog looked at me and pranced, yes pranced, toward the bakery. When we were in the nice warm confines of the back room, I lifted him up, removed his lead, and gave him a kiss on the head before putting him in the gated pen.

Trent reached down and scratched Bubba behind the ears. "Aren't you a lucky pup?"

His jacket slid off one shoulder, and I took it all the way off before handing it to him. "Thank you."

"Will you have dinner with me tonight?" When I remained silent, he turned to Bubba. "Don't you think Aunt Reese should have dinner with me?" As though the dog understood he looked at me and panted excitedly. "See? He agrees."

"I have a date." When his brows furrowed, I explained, "With my granddad."

His hand went to his chest as though relieved. *That was a bizarre reaction.*

"Oh, okay. I won't have any other free nights because of the big game coming up. Can I call you?"

I nodded. "Yes, of course."

Trent kissed my cheek. "I'll talk to you later. Give your grandfather my best." He started to walk away and my eyes decided to take in the view before me… and what a view it was. He closed the door behind him, and once again, I found myself confused over my new feelings for Trent Archer.

6

Trent

THE CHAMPION'S BOWL TROPHY WAS ours. We'd won the game and I couldn't wait to see Reese. She was somewhere in the stadium, I just wasn't sure where. After the award ceremony and several interviews, I headed to the locker room and celebrated with the coach and guys for a bit. Champagne flew into the air as popped corks sounded. We celebrated as a team, but realizing things weren't settling down, I changed into my street clothes and grabbed my phone. And despite the numerous texts waiting for me, hers was the first one I read.

> **Reese:** *Congratulations, MVP.*

I couldn't help but feel pride surge in my veins at that accolade. Although honored, I believed in the corny saying that there was no I in team. We all played a part. Jackson had an amazing game: one rushing touchdown, one receiving. Our wide receiver had one, and our kicker's foot was on fire tonight. His fifty-seven yard field goal to end the first half and put us up by ten was amazing. I couldn't forget our defense that had three sacks, a pick-six, and prevented more third down conversions than they had all year. That was why, in my acceptance speech, I was honest in saying I shared my trophy with my team.

My head was spinning, and my feet felt as though they were walking on clouds. We all started to leave the stadium, and as we were greeted by fans behind the gates, I replied to Reese's text message.

> *Thank you. Where are you?*

> **Reese:** *Alexa and I just left. We're at Tavern on the Hill. Enjoy your celebration.*

Damn it. She left.

> *Okay. Can I come by there?*

> **Reese:** *I'd bring a bodyguard if you do. There are several Rockets fans here. As a matter of fact, I'm starting to get itchy. *wink emoji**

> *Ha ha. Very funny. I'll be there soon and satisfy your itch.*

I knew how that sounded and didn't care. Just then, Jackson walked up to me and smacked me between my shoulder blades.

"Dude, I'm so stoked. Let's go celebrate. Look at all of the possibilities."

My eyes scanned the crowd behind the fencing. Fans were clamoring for autographs, selfies, and some were angling for something a bit more personal. Even in my earlier years, I wasn't into jersey chasers. Not that I'm old at the age of twenty-eight, but regardless, the only woman who piqued my interest was the beautiful, sassy, football-loving blonde waiting for me. Well, maybe not waiting, but I only wanted to see Reese.

"I'm going to meet Reese and Alexa at the Tavern. Want to come?" I saw the way Jackson looked at Alexa when we were in the bakery.

"Sure, sounds good."

We signed some autographs, mostly for kids, and headed to the players' parking lot. Jackson and I got into my SUV. Despite the game ending an hour ago, traffic was still a mess. Fans lined the streets, forcing cars to move at a snail's pace.

"So, you like Bird?"

"Bird?" I questioned.

"I mean, it fits."

Ignoring his nickname, I wasn't expecting him to ask that question. Did I like Reese? Yes, very much. I found her to be funny, smart, confident, and beautiful. She was also very outspoken, something I wasn't used to when it came to women. The only woman who ever held her ground with me was my mother.

When I realized Jackson's focus was still on me, I nodded. "Yeah, I do." Then I laughed. "She knows the weirdest football stats."

The traffic finally started moving and twenty minutes later, we pulled into the bar's parking lot. Jackson and I both slid on non-descript baseball caps in hopes it would aid anonymity. Reese hadn't been kidding when she said there were a lot of fans at the bar. If the crowd waiting to get in was an indication of what was happening beyond the wooden doors, we'd never have a moment's peace.

This wasn't going to work.

I plucked my phone out of my back pocket and shot Reese a text.

> Hey. Jackson and I are in the parking lot, but there's a crowd lined up to get in. Looks like they're waiting for us. Not sure we'll be able to slip in unnoticed.

Three little dots popped up.

> **Reese:** I'm currently rolling my eyes. LOL

I had to laugh at how I must have sounded. Before I could reply, another text came in.

> **Reese:** Did you want to go somewhere else?

My house. Do you girls mind coming over? We can hang out. I have a stocked bar.

Reese: *We took a car service here. Shoot me your address, and we'll meet you there.*

I'll drive us. Text me when you come outside, I'll pull up.

Reese: *Okay, leaving now.*

A few minutes later, her text arrived, and Jackson popped out of his side to open the back door. The girls slid in right as someone noticed him. Jackson gave a quick wave, hopped back in, buckled up, and we left.

It didn't take long to get to my place in Arlington. When I pulled into the older neighborhood, I watched Reese in the rearview scanning the surroundings. I knew her grandfather lived not too far from here. I pulled up to my driveway, punched in a code, and the gate swung open.

It may have seemed arrogant to some to live beyond a gate, but the sense of security it brought me put any arrogance to the side. I'm all for fans, but I also liked my privacy. I wasn't much into being in the limelight. But the gorgeous blonde in my backseat, who inadvertently turned us into a meme, hadn't help matters much.

After I parked, we all got out of the car. The girls were dressed casually, and although Alexa's eyes were wide, Reese didn't seem to be overly affected by my house — which I was more than happy about.

"I didn't know you lived so close to my granddad," she said, walking up to my front door.

"He's the one who told me about this neighborhood," I admitted. She nodded and I felt like a heel. Despite her beginning to soften around me, I had a feeling she'd hang on to the animosity of me signing with the opposing team rather than her grandfather. But I had my reasons. They were personal and nothing to do with the Thunder's organization. If they could have offered me a starting position and the same salary, I would have picked them.

We all walked inside, I tossed my keys on the small table in the foyer, and headed toward the kitchen. It seemed that Lily had been there, since my refrigerator was stocked with everything I'd need for the week. There wasn't much I splurged on, but having someone do my grocery shopping and tidying up for me while I was away didn't fall into that category. I enjoyed coming home to a clean house. Once the season was over, Lily would only come once a month rather than once a week.

"This is really nice."

"Thanks, Alexa. Would you like a wine or beer? I also could make you a drink if you'd like? Margarita?"

"Ooh, yes, a Margarita would be great. If it isn't too much trouble."

"No trouble at all." I looked at Reese who had been quiet. "Reese, what can I get you?"

"I'll have the same as Alexa, thank you."

Jackson helped himself to a beer and handed me one. Once the girls had their drinks, we went into my living room and made ourselves comfortable.

"So, what comes next?" Alexa asked, sipping her icy cocktail. "Disney World?" Her laugh made the rest of us chuckle.

"Well, we were just informed that Trent and I were selected to the All-Pro game in Phoenix."

Alexa beamed while Reese cringed. "What was that look?"

She startled and shook her head. "Nothing. I didn't have a look. I think it's great. Congratulations."

I couldn't stop my brows from furrowing. Something was off with her. Did Reese not think that we were deserving of going to the game? There were a couple players from the Thunder going as well. But there was definitely something in her eyes that didn't scream the same elation as her best friend showed.

"So, want to grab a snack?" Jackson asked Alexa, who nodded and followed him into the kitchen.

"Talk to me, Reese. We may not have known each other for long, but just as you know my tells,

I am getting a read on yours." She let out a breath. "Right there. When you do that, I know you have something to say, so go ahead and say it. It's not like you to hold back. Should I remind you of the day in the stands? If you've forgotten, I'm sure I can find the meme floating around."

"Fine, I'll tell you. I think those games are risky. I understand the accolade and the honor that goes along with playing at those games, but as I'd advise our players, unless you're willing to risk injury, take the nod that you were invited and go relax. Morgan, our tailback, got invited but declined. I know it's important to the league, it keeps marketing and ad money coming in, but in my lowly opinion, it isn't worth the possibility of getting hurt."

I'd heard that argument before when I played in college. Although then, I hadn't been around for those games. It would have been my senior year when I opted out of on-campus learning.

"I think you're being a bit dramatic. No one is out for blood."

She shook her head. "I disagree. Some of those guys are on their last year of their contracts and do have something to prove — all-pro or not."

"You're overreacting."

Reese shrugged and something told me she had stats tickling the tip of her tongue but she swallowed them and smiled. "You're right. I tend to be a worrier at times. You deserve a chance to play. You've earned it. Plus, you're a grown man. You can make your own decisions."

I nodded and tapped my bottle against her glass. "Thank you."

Jackson and Alexa returned. Her eyes ping-ponged between us. "Everything okay in here?"

"Yes, everything is fine." I glanced at everyone. "How about a game of pool?"

Alexa nodded. "That sounds like fun!"

"Umm, I don't know. We should probably get going soon."

"Nah, the night is young, Bird. And Trent is a pool wiz."

"Is he, now? And wait, did you just call me bird?"

Alexa laughed at Reese's question. Then she snapped her fingers. "I get it. Because she gave Trent the finger." Reese shook her head but didn't seem put off. "I know," Alexa continued. "Let's play boys against girls. Although we aren't very good, it'll be fun."

I exchanged a glance with Reese who looked as though she wanted to muzzle her friend. "What are we playing for?"

"How about if we win, you buy us dinner?" Alexa offered as a suggestion.

"Done. And if we win?" Jackson asked.

I knew what I wanted. And suddenly I felt as

though I were a teenager. All I wanted to do was kiss Reese, but that sounded ridiculous. Just as I was about to say something, Jackson chimed in, "Free cookies for a month."

He shook hands with Alexa, and Reese and I just stood there. I couldn't help but wonder if she wanted to change the stakes as much as I did.

7

Reese

I WALKED AROUND THE TABLE, twisting the blue chalky square on the tip of my pool cue. Trent was the last one to play, and I knew that he purposely set me up with a horrible shot. Alexa and I lost two games to Jackson and Trent. But they decided to sit this one out. So, it was me against the hot QB. Except he didn't know that for the first two rounds, I had held back.

After examining the felt, I figured out what I wanted to do. Setting the chalk down, I used the cue to point to the top of the table. "Six ball in the corner pocket." I bent over the side and lined up my shot. Trent came up behind me. Close enough that his thigh brushed up against my bottom. Craning my head, I looked at him. "Do you mind?"

"You're never going to make that shot without hitting the eight ball. You do know that if you hit it, you lose?" He paused. "On second thought, I do like cookies. Don't let me stop you."

And I had him just where I wanted him. Straightening, I turned and he took a step back. Cocking a brow, I asked, "Care to wager?"

A slow smirk crawled across his face. "We already have a bet going, but if you want to add to the ante… fine by me. What do you have in mind?"

"Loser kisses the winner," Alexa said.

"What are we? Twelve? And that makes zero sense." I was ready to throttle my friend, who merely shrugged at my question. Subtlety was not in her vernacular.

"Sex?" Jackson said, high-fiving a laughing Alexa. The pair had clearly had too much to drink.

"I'm fine with a kiss. Although, it doesn't matter if I lose." Trent leaned closer and breathed in my ear. "Because I'd still be the winner."

"No, think of something else." There was no way I could kiss him. But man, did I want to. Just not in front of our friends and not because of a game of pool. I shook my head. What was wrong with me?

"Okay, if you win, you can ask me anything, and I'll answer it."

"Anything?" He nodded. "Okay, and if I lose?"

"Then you answer a question."

"Fine."

We shook hands, and I shooed him away before lining up my shot. With one eye closed, I focused on the spot I needed to strike on the cue ball. It needed to be a delicate tap so I wouldn't scratch, but still strong enough for it to roll just right. Then all I needed to do was sink the eight ball, and I'd claim victory.

My right arm drew back before slowly moving forward. The balls knocking together sounded before sending the six-ball straight into the pocket, missing the eight ball by a fraction. Alexa clapped, I exhaled, Jackson laughed, and Trent cursed.

Not only had I sunk my ball, but I also left a straight path for the eight ball to easily slide into the opposite corner. I called my shot, sunk it, and hung up my pool cue.

"Bird's a hustler," Jackson chuckled.

I shrugged. "Granddad has a table at his house."

"Congratulations. What's your question?"

Ignoring Alexa's silent plea to remain quiet, I turned to Trent. "Why did you stand up Tracy Martin for the spring formal?" He blinked a few times as though I'd asked the question in a foreign language.

"I've never intentionally stood anyone up."

My jaw dropped. *Was he kidding?* It didn't

matter that it was almost five years ago. He should totally remember. The school made a huge deal about it. The fact that Trent acted oblivious annoyed me more.

"I had my reasons. It had nothing to do with her."

"What? You weren't there. She was devastated. You still didn't answer my question."

"And I'm not going to."

Knowing me well enough, Alexa slid off the stool she was sitting on and came to stand next to me. "Okay. That's fine. We're leaving."

Before I knew it, Trent grabbed my hand and pulled me out of the rec room and into the one next to it that appeared to be a small den.

"I'll tell you why I missed that dance. I was in California." That much I knew from the picture of him on a beach. He ran his hand through his hair, not caring a bit that he left it a bit disheveled and a lot sexy. "My mom was going through chemo. After that season ended, I went back to California to be with her."

I stood there feeling like the biggest loser on the planet. My heart cracked open not knowing if she was still alive. "I'm—"

Trent held up his hand stopping me. "For your information, and not knowing why this is so important to you, I ended up sending Tracy Martin two tickets to the Rockets' training camp. She came with her then boyfriend. After I treated them to dinner, all was forgotten, I was forgiven, and Tracy and her now husband became long time Rockets fans."

"I didn't know that. No one said anything."

"That's probably because no one knew. I didn't feel the need to publicize a nicety." After a few beats of silence, his brows pulled together. "Wait a minute, were you the one who answered the door that day when she got the roses?" I nodded. "Yeah, that was a pledge who had the misfortune of breaking the news. He told me a gorgeous blonde answered the door and looked as though she wanted to castrate him."

Pressure built behind my eyes. I'd never felt like a bigger bitch than I had at that moment. Not even when I gave him the finger. It was a wonder he even wanted to spend time with me. "I'm sorry." He nodded, but his lips remained in a fine line.

"Care to amend the bet?" I asked, wanting to do anything to make this better. Then again, why would he want to kiss me?

"Seems a bit late for that, but what did you have in mind?"

Rather than answer him, I took two steps toward him. My heart slammed against my ribcage. I'd never felt so forward in all of my life. The only time his eyes left mine were to flick to my lips. Not wanting my common sense to kick in, I rolled onto the balls of my feet, he leaned down, and brought my lips to his. It was a closed mouth kiss, but his hands went to my hips, mine to his strong shoulders. We stood there, mouth to mouth, the only noise was my pulse that had soared to my ears. When I broke our connection, his green eyes bore into mine.

"Trent... is your mom okay?"

"Yes, she's in remission. Thank you for asking." I nodded beyond grateful for that answer. "Are we good?"

He was asking me? "I think I should be asking you that question. After all, I was the one who assumed the worst of you."

"That is true..." He let his voice trail off. That gentle pause made me realize I wanted his answer to be yes. "I need to think about it."

Feeling my chest grow heavy, I gave a slight disappointed but understanding nod. "Oh, okay."

A cocky smirk appeared on his handsome face. "How about I give you my answer tomorrow night?"

With a slight tilt of my head, I studied him. "What's tomorrow night?"

"Our first date."

I should have known a man like Trent wouldn't easily give up. I'd be lying if I didn't admit there wasn't a part of me that was happy about that. Of course, I was the one who kissed him. I couldn't believe how wrong I'd been. Especially about the reason he never showed up all those years ago. Of course, there was still the issue about not signing with the Thunder, but that was a business decision. Personal life was a completely separate issue and, quite frankly, a more important one.

Tonight I'd be going on a date with Trent. Alexa and I sat in my room rummaging through my closet. She pulled out a little red dress. "What about this dress? Your legs would look amazing."

"No way. First of all, it's too short. Second, it's winter, and last, no."

She rolled her eyes and hung it back up. "Do you know where he's taking you?"

"He didn't say. Just that he was picking me up at seven."

"Okay." Alexa continued to slide the hangers in search of the perfect outfit, while I sat at my vanity applying mascara.

"Oh my gosh, the tag is still on these." When I looked up in the mirror and saw the black leather pants she had given me last Christmas, I shook my head. "You've had these for a year and have never worn them?"

I didn't want to hurt her feelings and tell her they weren't really me, so instead I said, "I haven't really had an opportunity to wear them."

"Well, now you do." She set them on the bed

and continued to pilfer through my clothes. When she pulled out a black off-the-shoulder sweater, I again shook my head.

"I'll look like Sandy in *Grease!*" She laughed, put it away, and continued her quest. "No leather pants tonight, please."

Once my lashes were lengthened and curled, I moved on to my hair. Deciding to wear it down, I ran my straightener through it a few times.

"Right. They may be hard to get off the first time you wear them. Remember like that episode in *Friends*? When Ross wore leather pants?" We both started to laugh. Then she blurted out. "Ahh! I got it!"

When I turned, I saw she laid out my short tan suede skirt, over the knee-high black suede boots with a heel not made for snow, a black turtleneck sweater, and textured tights. "What do you think? Sexy, but covered."

Did I want to look sexy? After giving it some thought, I nodded. "Okay."

Alexa clapped her hands. "He's going to swallow his tongue when he sees you in this." I crinkled my nose. "What? He is! And better access." When my eyes widened at the word *access,* she shrugged. "You should finish your makeup."

I glanced in the mirror. "I'm done."

"Sit down. I'll fix it."

Sighing, I did as she asked, and when my best friend swiped a nude gloss on my lips that somehow made them look plumper than they were, she stood back and nodded once. "Yeah, Trent isn't going to know what hit him. May I stay until he gets here?"

"No."

"You're no fun."

We laughed and once I promised not to wipe off any of her hard work, or change my outfit, she walked out. Fifteen minutes later my doorbell rang. I gave myself a once-over, grabbed my leather jacket, and pulled open the door.

Trent's eyes took a trip up and down my body. When they landed on my face he smiled. "Wow, you look incredible."

Blushing, I gave him my own once-over. As usual, he looked like every woman's fantasy. Black jeans and a gray crew neck sweater that for some reason made his eyes look like pools of liquid emeralds.

"You look pretty good yourself."

"Thanks. Are you ready?"

Ready as I'll ever be. "Yes."

With his hand on my hip, he leaned in and kissed my cheek, replacing the cool evening air with a flash of heat I felt between my legs.

Maybe I should have worn the leather pants.

8
Trent

REESE PARKER WAS HANDS DOWN the most gorgeous, surprising, and smartest woman I'd ever met. Legs that seemed to go on forever kept diverting my attention from her face. During every red light on the drive to my surprise location, I had to force myself to focus on the road. Even making idle chitchat seemed to be difficult. Thankfully, the drive wasn't too far and the music on the radio filled my quiet car.

When I turned the corner, our destination came into view. I glanced over at Reese. The bare trees mixed with the streetlights created dancing shadows on her face. Her hands nervously fidgeted with the strap of her purse.

"Hurlies?" The jovial lilt in her voice had me wondering if she'd been here before. "Is it closed?"

An honest question, considering there were only three cars in the parking lot including my own. The others I knew belonged to the owners and cook.

"Not exactly." I turned my car's engine off and hopped out to open her door, but she was already outside of it.

Technically, this was a date, and my hand went to reach for hers. Except, I didn't want to force the issue, so I settled for placing my hand on her back to guide her to the front door. A sign on it read, CLOSED FOR PRIVATE PARTY.

Reese turned and looked at me. Keeping quiet, I pulled the door open and guided her inside. Old wood flooring sounded hollow beneath our shoes. Her eyes scanned our surroundings; wood tables without any patrons, a hearty oak bar sat in front of twenty empty stools, and classic rock playing over the speakers. Aside from Tommy, the bartender and owner, and his wife, Carrie, we were the only ones in the large room. Reese's eyebrows drew together, causing a cute vertical line to form above the bridge of her nose.

Along with the chalkboard listing the beers on tap, a small bar menu, and a list of the teams who played in Hurlies' axe throwing league, were banners and posters of local teams including the Rockets and Thunder. Then on the wall next to a jukebox, was a framed signed jersey that I had given Tommy when he opened the bar.

"Come on," I once again, placed my hand on her back. Tommy smiled when we approached him. I shook his hand. "Hey, thanks for this."

"Anything for my favorite player. Congrats on the win and being named MVP." We fist bumped, and I could almost hear Reese's eyes rolling.

"Thanks, man. This is Reese. Reese, this is Tommy. He owns this great place with his wife, Carrie."

Reese held out her hand. "It's nice to meet you."

Tommy shook her hand just as Carrie came out from the back door. "Well, well, if it isn't Trent Archer."

"Hey, Carrie." I leaned in and kissed her cheek "Care, this is Reese. Reese, Carrie."

"It's a pleasure to meet you, Carrie. Cool place."

"Thank you. Well, it's all yours tonight thanks to this guy."

Reese pivoted and looked at me. "You rented this out for the night. Just for us?"

"Yes. I didn't want us to be bothered. Especially while you had an axe in your hand. I know you have a foul temper."

Not to mention I couldn't promise I wouldn't have throttled anyone who came on to her. In jeans, Reese Parker was gorgeous. In this short skirt and boots that were definitely made for a lot more than walking, she looked like every man's dream.

Her scowl was most likely due to my temper comment, yet she didn't refute it. "Fine, but just so you know, I'm a sweetheart around most people."

Tommy chuckled behind us, and when I turned around, he was giving me the okay signal with his hand. Carrie gave an approving nod as well. Rolling my eyes, I walked over to one of the stalls. Reese studied the diagram on how to properly throw an axe without harming either yourself or someone else in the process.

"Have you ever done this before?"

She shook her head, picking up an axe with her right hand. "No." Reese lifted the steel blade weapon a few times testing its weight. "It's lighter than I thought."

"It's designed for throwing not splitting wood. Unless you already know that and are an axe wielding hustler."

"Nope." I narrowed my eyes and studied her. "What? I'm not. All I can say is, I wouldn't stand too close."

Her slighted tone would have had me feeling like a heel if she hadn't hustled me during our pool game.

"Step aside, I'll show you a few things." Reese handed me the axe and moved off to the side. I stepped up to the line and glanced over my shoulder. Her right elbow rested on her left arm that was crossed over her chest, and she was nibbling on the side of her thumb staring at my backside in a trance-like state.

Smirking, I cleared my throat, and her eyes darted to mine. *Busted.* "It'll be more beneficial if you watch my arms. Not that I mind you checking me out."

She clucked her tongue against the roof of her mouth and crossed her arms. "Please. I was looking at your stance."

"Sure, whatever you say."

She let out an exasperated sigh as I lined up my body, faced the target, and began to explain the basics. With one foot forward, I raised the axe above my head, releasing it around eye-level, and watched it sail toward the target landing the blade dead center in the bullseye.

"Looks easy enough," she said, walking up to me with an axe in her hand.

When I stepped forward to retrieve mine, I glanced back and warned, "Don't throw yet."

Reese shook her head. "Good-looking and funny." Realizing the compliment that slipped from her mouth, she amended, "You know what I mean."

"Yes, that you find me sexy."

"I didn't say sexy."

I pulled the axe from the wooden board and walked toward her. Leaning close enough to feel the heat radiating from her skin, I breathed into her ear. "It's okay if you did, I find you extremely sexy."

She took a step back leaving one foot on the line. Her skirt rose on her toned thighs. With a look of concentration, Reese lifted the axe, closed her eyes, and let go. The top of the blade hit the wood with a loud thud before landing on the concrete floor.

"Ugh." Reese turned to look at where I was standing off to the side. "Can I try it again?"

"By all means."

For the next twenty or so minutes, Reese monopolized the stall, hitting the wood a few times before the axe clanked on the floor, but never the target. "What am I doing wrong?"

Walking up behind her, I handed Reese an axe which she gripped with her right hand then placed her left beneath it. Reaching around her waist, I placed my right hand over hers, and kept my left hand on her hip.

With her back to my front, I stepped off to the left. Her perfectly shaped ass leaned against my thigh. "Don't flick your wrist." I kept my hand wrapped around her dainty one. "When you lift your arm, look at where your elbow is pointing." I moved us back and forth letting her get the feel of the motion. "That *should* be the direction the axe goes. Let's do it together, ready? When I say, 'release,' let go of the axe. Don't hit me in the head." She glanced back with worry in her eyes. "I'm kidding."

"Okay."

In one swift motion, I helped her raise the axe, leaning enough away not to get clocked with it, and with a fluid stroke, brought it forward. "Release."

Our hands simultaneously left the rubber grip. We watched as the blade hit two rings south of the bullseye.

"I did it!" her squeal echoed. Reese turned, jumped up, wound her arms around my neck, and hugged me. Our height difference had me lifting her off the ground. Her joy made me just as happy. That's when an odd feeling washed over me. I always wanted to be the one responsible for putting that beautiful smile on her face.

We looked at each other and it took Herculean strength to not kiss her. Reese placed one of her hands on my chest as I slowly slid her down my body, lowering her until her feet rested on the floor.

"Ready to try it again?" She nodded and broke our connection. Handing her an axe, I stepped to the side. "Okay, show me what you've got."

Reese stepped up to the line, lifted the axe, then lowered it, and looked at me. "Thanks, Trent. This was a great first date."

"Sweetheart, it isn't over yet."

She blushed and tossed the axe, hitting the middle of the target. I shook my head, laughed, and wondered if there was anything this woman couldn't do. After her reaction the first time she'd hit the board, I didn't think she had hustled me, but even if she had, I didn't care because just a few minutes ago, I had Reese Parker in my arms.

Tommy dropped off three baskets of wings, small plates, an empty bowl, a pitcher of beer, and two frosty glasses. He walked away and we were once again alone. Reese's eyes widened when she saw the saucy chicken. After telling her I had ordered mild, medium, and hot, she immediately went for the fiery ones, and I couldn't help but smile.

She dug in and took a bite out of a drumette and moaned. "Wow." Her tongue poked out and swiped her lips before bringing the morsel back to her mouth. Once it was clean, she tossed it into the bowl and grabbed another of the same type. When her eyes landed on mine, she paused mid-chew. "Aren't you going to have any?"

I poured our beers and took a sip of mine before answering. "Yes, I am. Is there one you don't prefer? Or I can order more hot ones if you'd like."

"Thank you, but no. I'm afraid I'll eat them all. Did you know that wings are my weakness?"

Laughing I picked one up and set it on my plate. "I didn't. But good to know." I shot her a wink and stripped the bone in one bite.

"Do you prefer the flats or legs?"

"I don't like to discriminate. Legs... breasts... I like them all." I waggled my brows. Not seeming to be one bit affected, I amended my reply. "I like the flats better. You?"

She shrugged a shoulder. "Either is fine with me. Did you know the Buffalo chicken wing craze was created by accident?" When I shook my head, Reese nodded before taking another bite. "It's true or at least that's the story out of Buffalo."

"Do you know stats about everything?"

Reese laughed and put her stripped wing into the bowl. After wiping her hands, she took a sip of her beer. "Technically, that isn't a stat but rather a fun fact. But I do love stats. Some are so interesting. Most revolve around football, of course."

"How did that come to be?"

"Well, when you grow up in a family like mine, football is a way of life. When I was little, all I wanted was to be with my granddad. We'd watch games, and I'd get so confused at the different plays and rules. Kenzie seemed to get it right away. I needed to think of a way to remember things. It's like spelling. For example, desert versus dessert. I remember that dessert has two Ss because so does the word ass." When I continued to stare, not understanding where her logic was going, she added, "If I eat a lot of dessert, my ass will get bigger."

I let out a loud chuckle. "I never thought about it that way. For the record, I like your ass just fine." Unsurprisingly, she rolled her eyes at me. But the blush that tinged her cheeks contradicted any animosity she may have toward me. "Okay, what else? Give me a football stat I don't know."

Taking her time to dip a wing into the little plastic cup of blue cheese dressing and taking a bite, she swallowed and nodded. "Did you know that Carlisle from the Gladiators completes more passes when the temperature is below sixty-two degrees? And his completion percentage goes up by seven percent if those games are played on artificial turf?"

"No, I didn't know that." I had to ask what I'd been wondering. "Do you have any fun facts about me?"

Her face took on a reddish hue. "Well, aside from the obvious, that you excel at home, in games where you win the coin toss, you have more passing yards than those when you lose the toss." *Huh. That was something I didn't know.* "Also, you have more passing yards on odd weeks. So, if I were the opposing defensive coordinator, I'd run a nickel defense more often than not."

Clearly thinking she just handed me the holy grail and spilled the Thunder's secret playbook, her eyes widened. Once again hearing her talk football had to be one of the biggest turn-ons. "Anything else?"

"Nope," she quickly said, popping the P at the end. She leaned back in her chair and let out a breath. "I'm stuffed."

I stood and offered her my hand, which she took, sending an odd sensation up my arm. If I didn't know better, I would have thought I slammed my elbow on the table. It was *that* type of tingle. Her eyes connected with mine, and I wondered if she felt it too.

I wasn't sure what was happening, but I knew she was responsible for it.

9

Reese

WHAT WAS THIS MAN DOING *to me?* I flexed and wiggled my fingers to try and alleviate the odd sensation. The same one I felt when I threw myself into his arms and Trent's eyes locked onto mine. When I put my hand on his hard chest, his heart beat fast and strong beneath my palm. Knowing that I had been the reason for that, turned me on in a way I hadn't expected — he wasn't what I had expected.

Trent definitely had a way about him. I suppose it was because of what he did for a living. A lot of people think football players are nothing but muscular bodies slamming into others made of the same. Except, I knew that was the furthest thing from the truth. Aside from their brawniness and hard hits, they each had a job to do.

On the field, Trent, like every other quarterback, was the leader. He was in charge of executing plays and making changes based on how the opposing team reacted to where everyone had lined up. In turn, his team would protect him to insure he wouldn't get injured, and he'd do the same.

Trent had to be smart. Methodical. Prepared. All of which he seemed to be in his private life. Even the way he threw the axe had been done with precision. And just like on the field when he threw a football, it seemed effortless. I'd also need to be blind not to notice his physique beneath his clothing. As gorgeous as he was in a football uniform, he was equally stunning in jeans and a sweater—maybe even more so.

Everything I'd thought I knew I wanted or in this case, didn't want, seemed to be flying out the window. There was zero doubt when I went to bed tonight and let my lids slide closed, that I would be able to feel his strong warm hands wrapped around me, his chest against mine, and the way his body tensed beneath my touch.

"Reese?"

His deep voice pulled me from my thoughts. "I'm sorry, what?" He had my jacket in his hands, holding it open for me. "Oh, thank you." I slid it on and pulled my hair from beneath the collar.

"I had asked if you would like to go grab a coffee."

"Oh, I'm getting a little tired."

We started to walk out but not before saying goodbye to Tommy and Carrie who had invited us back anytime. Trent thanked them before we stepped out into the nighttime air. A shiver ran through me and before I knew it, Trent's arm swung around my shoulder.

"Smells like it's going to snow again."

"Snow smells?" I swallowed my laugh when I glanced up at his serious expression.

"I'm surprised you didn't know that. Don't tell me you don't know any sensational snow statistics."

"Say that five times fast." I couldn't stop the giggle from flying out of my mouth before sharing a fun fact. "A football game hasn't been postponed or cancelled due to snow since 1933."

Trent shook his head, then catching me off guard, he kissed my temple. Neither of us said a word, he just opened the door for me, I slid into his car and waited for him to do the same. He pushed a few buttons and within a few minutes my seat warmed.

"Better?"

"Yes, thanks. So, when do you leave for Arizona?"

"Sunday. Then we'll have daily workouts and practice as a team before the game next week." When I remained quiet he added, "Then we'll have a fan day. All profits go to a children's charity."

I knew that and quite frankly, that was the only positive about the game. "Well, at least you'll be warm."

"Why don't you come with me?" My head snapped to the left. Trent's eyes flicked to mine before focusing on the road. "Isn't your grandfather going?"

"No, he isn't. Dave and Kenzie will be there. Shoot, I forgot I'll have Bubba. I really hope it doesn't snow. He loves it."

Trent chuckled. "That's a bad thing?"

"Yes, have you ever tried to get snowballs out of a Bichon's fur?"

"Can't say that I have."

"Well, it's not fun."

We pulled into my driveway. Trent put the car in park and looked at me. "I had a great time tonight. Thank you for going with me."

Before I knew it, "Would you like to come in?" flew out of my mouth.

"I'd love to."

Our laughter filled my living room as Trent told stories of traveling with the team. I'd heard some stories, accidentally of course, at a couple Thunder parties, but hearing Trent talk about them took them to a different level.

"Troy is the saint of the group. I think it's because he's a rookie and doesn't want to cause waves. But the ladies love him."

"I'm sure they love all of you." His right eyebrow arched. "Don't tell me you all don't have a harem of women around you." As soon as that statement, not even a question, flew from my mouth, I regretted it.

"No, we do," he stated matter-of-factly.

Meanwhile, a swirl of jealousy—something I tried to avoid—flowed through me. It was dumb because I'd seen the pictures. I wouldn't call each one of them supermodels, but they definitely were beautiful. "Sounds like fun."

"It can be. But it gets old quick." I snort-laughed into my coffee mug. "You don't believe me?"

"Actually, I do, but I've been around enough players through the years to know what happens. I can't say that the blame is all on you guys. I've seen women literally throw themselves at a man just because he's a professional athlete. Is that why you're single?"

"No, I'm single because I choose to be. I didn't think I wanted a relationship. I'm also not a serial dater as the media likes people to believe. Do I date? Of course, but not in the traditional sense. Not until you. Going to a charity event isn't a date in my opinion... axe throwing is."

Trent winked and a warm chill scurried down my spine. "It was fun."

"Wait until our next date."

"What makes you think we're going on another one? You haven't even asked me."

He shifted on the sofa, leaned forward, and tucked a few strands of hair behind my ear before cupping my left cheek with his strong calloused hand. Our eyes locked. "I like you, Reese Parker. And I'd like to take you out again before I leave for Arizona. Then when I get back, we can pick up where we left off. What do you say? You're single, I'm single, let's not be single together."

"What are you asking?"

"To give me a chance. As you can see, I'm loads of fun. And in a way, you owe me."

A half-chuckle mixed with a huff flew from my mouth. "Owe you? How do you figure that?"

"Well, for one, you held something that happened five years ago against me without knowing the entire story. Two, you gave me the finger and turned us into a meme." I rolled my lips between my teeth to not giggle at that one. Not that I enjoyed being a meme, but dang, I'd be lying if I said that flipping him off hadn't felt fantastic.

"I said I was sorry about what happened with Tracy. In my defense, I didn't know you made it up to her. All I knew was how sad she was. Technically, not my fault." I paused a beat. "I'll give you that I'm a bit of a hothead, but that kiss and wink set me off. You should have been on the Thunder."

As soon as that left my mouth, I wanted to reel it in. "Is that why you did what you did? You know I had my reasons and respect the hell out of your grandfather. It wasn't personal, it was business."

"You sound like Tom Hanks in *You've Got Mail.*"

"Well, he was right."

I waved my hand back and forth doing my best to clear the air. Going into the details of how the Thunder needed a player of his caliber, wasn't any of his business. Quite frankly, he knew that.

"Regardless, I don't date football players." He smiled and a tiny window in my heart opened up… *and* a little voice in my head, which sounded a lot like Alexa, told me I'd be dumb to turn him down.

"Feel like making an exception?" His green eyes still tethered to mine, sparkled.

"I don't know, maybe."

"Can I try and convince you?"

The smolder in his eyes held me captive. When they flicked to my lips, I didn't bother to ask how he planned on convincing me because Trent came closer, paused as though he waited for me to pull away. When I didn't, his fingers slid into my hair, and he very gently brought his lips to mine. The first kiss he gave me was featherlight, teasing my senses. Tempting my willpower.

I could feel my resolve going up in smoke. The gentle coaxing of his kisses flipped a switch in me. A sudden surge of heat mixed with sensuality rushed through my veins. I couldn't stop my hands from running up his taut muscular torso, and fisting his cotton shirt to bring us closer together.

What was I doing?

"Reese," he whispered against my cheek, then my neck, before landing once again on my mouth. We moved in a perfect rhythm before I let go of him and we broke apart. His soft lips were a bit puffier and wore a sheen of my lip gloss that neither of us bothered to wipe away.

"I should go." Feeling lightheaded, we both stood. I'd blame my slight wobble on the boots, but I knew it was the man next to me who caused it.

Trent slid on his jacket and when we got to the door, he turned to me. "Can you take tomorrow afternoon off? I have a workout in the morning, but if you can swing it, there's someplace I'd like to take you."

"It shouldn't be a problem."

"Great." He opened the door and, before walking out, turned to look at me. His eyes roamed my body from head to toe and back up again. "Tomorrow, wear something more comfortable. Don't get me wrong, you look sexy as hell, and believe me when I say, it took every ounce of stamina not to ask to see what was under that skirt."

I felt myself blush at his forward compliment. "Okay, want to tell me where we're going?"

"No, it's a surprise." He chastely kissed my lips before tossing me that wink of his. "You know, I like this side of you much better."

"Yeah, yeah… I know." Not wanting to test my resolve, I closed the door, and brought my fingers to my lips. Never in my life had I been kissed like that. Nor had I ever kissed a football player.

It figured that Trent Archer, of all people, was my exception. All I could hope was that I didn't regret it.

10

Trent

I COULDN'T REMEMBER A TIME in my life when I veered off course. Maybe it was because I'd always followed a playbook. Since I was eleven years old, I've had a strict regimen—wake up, work out, go to school, go to practice, study, sleep. Naturally, I'd eaten in between. During my teenage years, parties and girls came into the mix, but I still kept my commitment to the sport of football.

Now, as I skipped rope to keep up my stamina, my mind wandered to kissing Reese. Last night she tasted of coffee and desire. There would be no denying the palpable chemistry between us. Nor was there zero doubt in my mind she didn't feel it as much as I had. I had a sense that even if she wasn't dog-sitting, she'd say no to going to

Arizona. And truth be told, I surprised myself by inviting her, but the thought of her with me, stirred up my libido. So much so, I almost wished I'd turned down participating.

It didn't matter that this weekend's game held no significance, it was still a competition. Any time an athlete put on a uniform and stepped onto the field, it was a battle. The trophy at the end meant nothing—winning did. Except, this weekend's game there was an understanding between the players. No one was out for blood. It wasn't a regular season game that meant your team would advance or get a bonus. The All-Pro was a game between the Eastern and Western Conferences. Some of the guys hadn't played together or against one another since college. That was what made it fun.

I flicked my wrists, sending the rope to circle my body three more times before I stopped jumping, thus ending my cool down. I grabbed my bottle of water and took a long swig. Jackson walked over with a towel slung around his neck, using it to wipe his forehead then his face. "Are you ready?"

Nodding, I tossed my now empty bottle into the recycle bin. "Yeah, I'm good. What about Troy?"

"He has a meeting with his agent this morning."

Troy was my backup but had the talent to be a starter. The kid had great speed. During high school, he lettered in both football and track. When he went to college, he was nominated for more than one athletic award. He knew the game, loved to strategize, and was humble. Despite being second to me, Troy never held any animosity. Instead, he watched and learned. Inevitably, another team would prosper from that knowledge.

I nodded. "I'm not surprised."

"Me neither. It's not like you're going anywhere. Although you are a free agent. Has Jasper sent you a new contract yet?"

Sam Jasper was my agent who was about to make me the highest paid quarterback in the league. After winning the Champion's Bowl, there was little to no doubt that I could write my ticket with the Rockets. That being said, there were a couple of other teams tossing their hats into the ring.

"We're meeting next week to go over the offer from the Rockets before accepting any others."

"I'm sure they'll come to an agreement. All hell would break loose if the Rockets released you. Can you even imagine? The MVP no longer playing for DC? Won't happen."

Hearing him say that made my stomach turn. I've known players who left winning organizations and vice versa. Playing for DC has been a highlight of my career, and as far as I was concerned, I planned on retiring as a Rocket.

We each took a quick shower, grabbed our

things from the locker room, and headed to the diner down the road. People usually recognized us, but most were adults who respected our privacy. Either that, or they wanted to eat their breakfast in peace before going to work.

It didn't take long for the waitress to come by and take our orders. We'd been ordering the same meals for years. Fifteen minutes later, she set down enough food to feed a family of six rather than two men, but after a workout, we always loaded up on protein.

Jackson took a bite of his steak. "How's the girlfriend?"

"I don't have a girlfriend." *Yet.*

He shook his head. "Fine. Let me rephrase: how's Reese? Is she still giving you the finger any chance she gets?"

"Funny and no. Saw her last night and will be seeing her later today."

"Ex-excuse me..." A young voice interrupted us. When I turned my head, a boy looked to be about seven or eight years old stood at the side of our table. "Aren't you Twent Archah and Jackson Cawtwright?" His adorable little-boy lisp had us both grinning.

A woman rushed over and put her hands on his shoulders. "I am so sorry. Connor saw you both and got excited. He's a big fan."

"Yowah biggest," he added.

It was then I noticed a notebook and black marker in his hand. "What' cha have there?"

"My math notebook. We're wearning take aways. I was wondering if you could sign it. I don't think my math teacher, Mrs. Hollis will cawah. She says you two are the weason she lets her husband watch football." Connor shrugged, and his mom blushed.

I glanced at Jackson who smirked. "Well, how about this... can I borrow your marker?" He handed it to me, I took off my baseball cap with our team's logo on the front and flipped it over. I signed the bill before handing it and the marker to Jackson who did the same.

"There you go, buddy." Jackson handed him the hat.

"Wow! This is so coow! No one's gonna bewieve this happened."

His mother cleared her throat. "Honey, let's let these nice men get back to their breakfast."

"Would you like a picture?" I asked, looking at his mother who immediately pulled her phone out of her pocket. Jackson and I scooted forward, and with us sitting and Connor standing, we were the same height.

"Okay, on the count of three say, Rockets." We all followed her instructions. Connor's Wockets made my smile grow wider. The kid was adorable. "Thank you so much, you made his day. But we should be going since he does have a little bit of studying to do and an errand to run."

"Yeah, we have a math quiz and if she's in a bad mood it will be one that's out wowd." He shivered. "I hate those."

Jackson took Connor's notebook and scribbled something in it before handing it to me. I laughed when I saw what he wrote.

To the best math teacher ever. He signed his name, and I did the same. I handed him back the book and when he saw it he thrust his hand in the air. "Yes! No way will she be in a bad mood now."

"Thank you so much," his mom said, placing a hand on her son's shoulder. "Connor, we need to get going if you still want to stop by Sugarcoat This."

We said our goodbyes, and while Jackson went back to devouring his meal, I grabbed my phone, and found the number for the bakery.

"Sugarcoat This, Alexa speaking. How may I make your day sweeter?"

"Hi, Alexa, it's Trent Archer."

"Um… hi, Trent. Reese isn't here. She had a meeting with her grandfather and is off this afternoon, but you know that."

Hmm… she told her about our date. Nice. "Thanks, but I'm not calling for Reese. A mother and son will be coming there this morning. His name is Connor, about seven or eight years old, and is wearing a red puffy winter jacket. Can you please box up a couple dozen cookies for them on me? Feel free to add whatever else they want. I can give you my card."

"For sure I can do that. No worry about your card, you can pay the next time you're here. I know you're good for it."

"Thanks, Alexa. Have a good day."

"Yeah, you too. And have fun this afternoon."

I swore I heard her giggle before my screen returned to the homepage.

Jackson looked up and shook his head. "Such a softy. Anyway, what do you have planned for your date?"

"Like I'd tell you."

Ignoring his glare, I dug into my breakfast, counting down the minutes until I would see Reese again.

The afternoon was perfect for what I had planned. Like I had predicted, it snowed overnight, leaving what looked like tiny diamonds scattered on the yards. I slid on my navy beanie, my favorite gray quarter-zip pullover, and headed over to Reese's house. Seconds after I pulled into her driveway and got out of my car, she opened the front door.

"Hi! Come on in." I stepped into her foyer, closing the door behind me. It was then I noticed she had on black leggings, and a long-sleeve white

T-shirt with the Thunder's logo on the front. Her blonde hair was pulled back into a ponytail.

"I wasn't sure where we were going. You said, casual, is this okay?"

"Do you realize how gorgeous you are?"

Reese's otherwise creamy skin turned rosy. "Thank you." She let her eyes travel the length of my body. "You look good too."

"Great. Grab a jacket, gloves, and whatever else you need. Our date is outside."

Her brows furrowed. "That's all you're telling me?"

Teasing her had quickly become one of my favorite past times. "Yes." She let out a small huff before grabbing a red knit cap, putting it on, and when she pulled her ponytail through a hole on the top, I laughed. "Clever."

Not being able to resist, I took a step forward and tucked a few errant strands of her hair into her cap letting my hand linger on her face just as I did last night. The need to kiss her was fierce, so I leaned down and did just that. It was chaste, just a peck, but for now, it would be enough.

Reese didn't object, instead she smiled, slid on a pair of black suede boots, grabbed her keys, and slung a small bag across her body. "I'm ready."

Side by side, we walked out to my car. The entire drive she stared out the window, watching the signs on the highway.

"Alexa told me what you did today." When I remained silent, she went on to say, "The cookies for that boy's class. And he told her that you gave him your hat after you and Jackson signed it."

"Oh, that. Right. Cute kid."

"Not many people would be so kind. I know players who, despite needing their fans, can be rude toward them. It's sad, really."

"I'd never do that." Out of my peripheral vision, I saw her staring at me. "What?"

"Nothing, you just continue to surprise me. Speaking of—"

She batted her eyelashes doing her best to look coy. Or maybe it was sweet and innocent. "Nice try. Although, you're adorable, I'm still not telling you." There really wasn't a reason for me to keep our destination to myself other than to bug her. It seemed we enjoyed doing that to one another.

She remained silent until I took the next exit. A couple turns later and she gasped. Like a kid who shook their Christmas gift until they figured out what was in the box, she screeched, "We're going ice skating?"

I couldn't tell if that tone in her voice was good or bad. "Yes, is that okay? If not—"

"No, it's great. Thank you. Wow, I haven't been here since I was a kid. Kenzie and I used to go sledding here too."

With the car barely in park, Reese was out the

door and looking at me. She bobbed on the balls of her feet, reminding me of a little kid getting ready to play in the snow for the first time.

"Would you like to do that instead?"

"Oh, no. It's fine. Ice skating is one of my favorite things. Plus, I think soaring down a hill or mountain isn't allowed per your contract." When my eyebrows rose, she amended, "We have a stipulation in our players' contracts about extreme sports. Not that sledding at Whisper Woods Park is extreme, but you know what I mean. Off season injuries could impact the team's success."

Reese was absolutely correct. The Rockets did add similar verbiage to my deal. "Well, we're just going ice skating. Nothing too extreme about that. Unless of course I trip and break an ankle."

"Poo, poo, poo," she blurted right before she fake spat on the ground and made the sign of the cross.

"What was that?"

"Don't jinx yourself!"

Laughing, I placed my hand between her shoulder blades. "Okay, thanks for warding off evil spirits."

In all seriousness, she acknowledged relief in her voice. "You're welcome."

Together we walked to the stand, got our skates, and laced them up. Reese stood as though she was just on them yesterday. I, on the other hand, wobbled a bit. We both laughed, and she held out her glove-covered hand. "Come on, I've got you."

It was a small gesture, but one that had me hanging on to her. The rink wasn't full, thanks to it being a school day. A few guys looked as though they were practicing for a hockey game. But mostly, the rink was empty.

Music filtered in from the outdoor speakers. Reese turned and was skating backward, taking both of my hands in hers. I had the feeling she was holding out on me. When the music turned to a rock ballad, Reese glanced behind her.

"Don't let me stop you."

A bright smile split her face in two. Reese let go of my hands and began to go around the rink like a pro. I skated off to the side and watched as she moved to the beat. The guys who were playing stopped to watch her as well. Part of me—a big part of me—wanted to tell them to keep their eyes to themselves. Except, the truth was, I couldn't blame them because Reese Parker was beautiful standing still. But the way her leggings hugged her curves as she glided across the ice was something different all together.

She was the entire package. I still wasn't sure if she'd let me be her exception, but I'd keep trying until she would.

11

Reese

MUCH TO MY GRANDMOTHER'S DISMAY, my granddad and I turned their dining room into a mini conference room, picking up from where we left off from our previous meeting.

On the drive over, I passed Trent's street and part of me wondered if he was home. That thought threw me for a loop. I couldn't remember when I thought of a man that way. My previous boyfriend, if you wanted to call him that, hadn't lasted very long. Actually, none of the guys I went out with made it past one or two dates. It hadn't been because they were dull, but I seemed to be more popular during football season.

Then there were the players. No one who played for the Thunder dared to ask me out. One, they respected the hell out of my granddad and wouldn't even consider crossing that line. Two, and probably the more obvious reason, they didn't want to break the heart of the owner's granddaughter. That one always irked me. Why would *my* heart get broken? Newsflash, it wouldn't because I didn't date football players.

As though he could read my mind, Granddad shifted a paper around and asked, "How's Trent?"

I let my hands fall to the tabletop and breathed out a long, full-of-confusion breath. "I don't know, Grandad. He's so perplexing, charming, and although his cocky confidence is sort of a turn-on, it's also one of the reasons why I didn't like him to begin with. In his defense, I came to the wrong conclusion back in college, but really, no one could blame me for that. So, I did feel awful, because I'm generally not one to jump to conclusions. Then..." I couldn't prevent sighing. "We went axe throwing, and he took me ice skating. Then he kissed me and everything started to shift. The man is beyond infuriating, yet can be sweet, kind, and... charming."

"Yes, you've said that already."

Glancing up, the old man—well, he was only in his sixties, so not terribly old—had a snarky grin on his face. It dawned on me that I just spilled my guts to my granddad. And even worse, I told him that Trent kissed me. Seriously, even when he wasn't in the near vicinity, Trent Archer made me lose my mind. Blood rushed to my brain and if I wasn't sitting, I may have toppled over.

My granddad's eyes never left mine. Nor did the smirk fall away from his face. This poor man had endured both of his granddaughter's teenage years. I supposed this was no different. Well, that wasn't completely true. When it came to my adolescent years, I didn't date too much. Having ties to one of the hometown teams made it impossible for me to distinguish between boys with genuine feeling for me or the Virginia Thunder.

"Sorry, Trent flusters me. Even when he's not here."

"He's a good man, Reese. Look at how he handled your little outburst."

Remorse caused my immediate frown. "I'm sorry about that. Truly. It's just he annoyed the hell out of me."

Granddad chuckled. "Well, at least it all turned out for the best. Now, how about we go through these player profiles that Marty from scouting sent over."

After spending almost two hours looking at statistics, my eyes began to glaze over. He must have noticed because he patted my hand and began to shift paperwork into piles. "I think we're done for now. I'll go over your comments with Terrance once he's back from Maui."

Terrance was the team's GM and, although he didn't want to leave, his niece was getting married in the tropics. He had been the one to send Granddad most of the profiles. He'd probably be on speaker phone with us right now if he thought his wife wouldn't kill him.

"Sounds good." I gathered my phone and notebook, and slid them into my oversized leather bag.

"What about Archer?" *Yes, use his last name Granddad, that will disassociate the gorgeous quarterback for a hot second.* "He's a free agent."

The thought of Trent being part of the Thunder's organization sent a thrill through me. And at the same time, brought upon a bout of nerves. Pushing my feelings aside, I answered as I would if he were any other player and not the one who invaded my brain throughout the day.

"First, I don't see the Rockets not re-signing him. I also don't see Trent walking away from DC unless he was given a very lucrative deal. I'm not sure making the necessary sacrifices to cover that amount would be beneficial for the team. On the other hand, there's Troy Davis. If Trent stays with the Rockets, Troy will most likely leave. He's too good to be a backup. Maybe if Trent was older, but the guy is in his prime." *Lord, was he ever.* "Anyway, I'd make a play for him." Granddad rested his chin on his fisted hand, appearing to be deep in thought. "Want to know what my plan would be?"

"So we're back to talking about business now?" He chuckled, probably because my face reddened, but I couldn't help but do the same.

"Yes, well, the Rockets need a kicker and a cornerback. As do, North Dakota and Iowa. North Dakota has already traded with Mississippi for another first round pick. Thanks to their losing season, North Dakota will be going first, and since DC will be picking last in the draft, getting who they want may be an issue. I know you know all of this, but I would trade our first round pick to DC in exchange for Davis. You might need to throw in another concession, but I'd start there."

He nodded and smacked his hand on the table. "Good idea. We'll schedule a meeting late next week and go over everything with Terrance and his staff."

I kissed him goodnight and found Grandma in the main room. "Drive safe, honey."

"I will. Thanks for dinner, it was great."

"Anytime, you know that. You make him very happy, you know." When she glanced toward the dining room, my eyes couldn't help but follow her sightline. Granddad was smiling and jotting things down on a piece of paper. *So much for being tired.*

"I'm glad to help. Love you."

She walked me to the door and as soon as it clicked closed behind me, I couldn't help but tip my head back and inhale the crisp nighttime air. The stars dotted the sky, the moon shone brightly, and everything seemed perfect.

Grabbing my phone out of my pocket, I saw a

missed text from Kenzie, reminding me she'd be dropping Bubba off in the morning. I swear my sister thought I had the memory of a hamster. Because of that, I decided to have a bit of fun.

> *What's tomorrow? I decided to get away for a bit. I'm at a spa in West Virginia.*
>
> ***Kenzie:*** *You are not. I just talked to Grandma.*
>
> *You're no fun. Yes, I know I'm watching my nephew for the week. I'm sure he's very excited about it. He loves me.*
>
> ***Kenzie:*** *Yes, I know he does. We'll see you in the morning.*
>
> *OK. Love you.*
>
> ***Kenzie:*** *Love you too, you weirdo.*

I laughed and tossed my phone into my bag before sliding into my car and heading home.

"Explain it to me again," Alexa stated, sounding bored. "The game doesn't mean anything, yet all the best players are there? Wouldn't they rather be in Bali or the Maldives?"

The two of us sat on my couch, drinking our traditional margaritas and enjoying the charcuterie tray the deli next to the bakery put together for us. Bubba lay in his cushy bed, gnawing on his favorite bone stuffed with peanut butter.

Her question was something I always wondered as well. I mean, I understood the honor of being named to the All-Pro team, but it should be just that. A player is added to the roster, it goes on his stat record, and no one is the wiser. Except, I'd yet to come across a player who agreed with my thought process.

"They're the best in the game playing against each other to see if the Eastern Conference is better than the Western one."

"Men," she said befittingly. "Ooh, there's Trent."

A beautiful brunette stood next to him, holding a mic in her right hand. I recognized her as Casey McGrath, a local pageant queen turned sports reporter from the DC Area. Her dark hair was pulled off her face in a low ponytail, and she wore a powder blue sweater making her light eyes almost look gray.

Meanwhile, Trent looked as sexy as sexy could be. His dark tousled hair, scruff covered jaw line, and lips I knew were soft and kissable, made him look sexier than he ever had. He smiled at her, and I was pretty sure Casey wasn't oblivious to his charms.

"Thank you for taking the time to speak with us, Trent." He nodded while sporting that glorious smile of his. "First, congratulations once again on bringing the Champion's Bowl Trophy home to DC."

"Thank you, Casey. It wasn't just me, the team worked hard and fought some tough gridiron battles."

She placed her left hand on his bicep and my eyes automatically narrowed at the familiar gesture. "Yes, of course. And now you're here at the All-Pro game. Not that there was any doubt in my mind that you wouldn't be."

"Did she just bat her eyes at him?" Alexa's nose crinkled. "And her hand hasn't left his arm." I'd be lying if I didn't acknowledge that they seemed very familiar with one another. Assuming my bestie's question had been rhetorical, I didn't bother to answer. "Well, I suppose he is single." Her gaze flicked to mine at the same time mine flicked to hers. "Admit it, Reese, you like this guy."

As soon as I was about to answer, Casey said, "Good luck today. At least there won't be any scorned fans, or in that case, relatives of the opposing team's owners in the stands who will end up in a meme with you."

Alexa gasped, I glared, and Trent smirked. Then, his pretty eyes found the camera.

"Shame isn't it? Bubba's a lucky fella." A whistle blew, and he winked at the lens before sliding his helmet on.

"Oh my God!" Alexa screeched. "Did he just say Bubba?"

My dog-nephew's head sprung up at the sound of his name. I refocused on the television. Casey said something about not understanding what that meant, but she laughed it off. There had definitely been something in the way she touched his arm, and I swore she looked a bit put off at his comment.

After the commercial break and the national anthem, the game started. Some of the guys looked as though they were out for blood. This game had always grated on my nerves, so maybe it was an exaggeration on my part.

Trent had the ball, dropped back in the pocket, and found a wide-open receiver. He let the ball fly, and connected with his teammate who ran the ball past mid-field. They huddled and Alexa sighed into her drink.

"Seriously, I love football. I don't understand much of it, but geesh! Look at them." We both laughed. "You're so lucky. Trent is beyond into you. When are you going to admit that you're into him too? You can't tell me that man doesn't make your toes curl in your favorite suede boots."

Letting out a breath, I admitted, "You're right. I am starting to fall for him. When we kissed it was unlike any other. I know how ridiculous that sounds, but that doesn't make it less true. We do like each other—"

"Wait, you kissed?"

Blushing, I glanced at the screen, and Trent

lined up behind his center. I watched the defense, and that was when I saw Beckett, a lineman who played for Austin, and had just lost against the Rockets, shift. "He's going to blitz," I voiced. Trent had the ball in his hands, he dropped back to pass. My heartbeat spiked, and I felt the lump in my throat grow as I saw it play out right before my eyes. "Look out!" I yelled, making Alexa jump and Bubba scurry across the room.

Then it happened. Trent released the ball, and Beckett charged at him, dropped his shoulder, and slammed into Trent right below his knees taking him to the turf. My hand flew to cover my mouth as I bolted off the couch. Alexa stood next to me as we both stared at the screen. Trent on the ground grabbing his leg, the refs tossing yellow flags into the air, the announcers stating the obvious that it was a roughing the passer foul; it all happened all at once.

A flurry of activity ensued from the coaches to the refs, to the team's medical staff, and the players taking a knee. But my sole focus was on Trent, thanks to the cameraperson capturing the anguished grimace that marred his otherwise gorgeous looks through his facemask.

Alexa squeezed my hand. Trent closed his eyes, and tears swelled in mine.

The network cut to a commercial. I stood staring at a dancing polar bear wondering if Trent knew how much he meant to me. Because if I hadn't realized it before the game, I sure as hell did now. Then again, if I didn't know, how could he possibly?

My cell phone rang and when I saw Kenzie's name, I grabbed it. "Kenz?"

"Hey, I wanted to let you know that Trent is being taken inside for evaluation. It appears that he has dislocated his patella." I closed my eyes, knowing that was the injury that plagued him in college. Not career ending at the time, but depending on the severity, it totally could be. "They'll also be putting him through concussion protocol. It was quite a hit."

A shiver ran up my spine at the thought of his head landing on that hard turf. "Okay, thank you for telling me. We went on two dates, you know."

"Yes, Granddad told me. I won't yell at you now for keeping your big sister in the dark." I half-smiled but hardly felt it.

"Will you call me when you know more?"

"Yes. Try not to worry."

Yeah, right. "Thanks for calling."

Casey was reporting from the sideline, explaining to the announcers in the booth the same thing Kenzie had just told me. I fell back onto the couch and turned toward Alexa. Her eyes looked as sad as I felt. "He'll be okay."

I nodded, said a silent prayer, closed my eyes, and whispered, "He has to be."

Trent

HEAT SOARED, NOT JUST THROUGH my veins, but my bones. The pain had been instant and it felt as though my shin had snapped, but I knew better. It was my knee... again. I'd endured hard hits before, but this one felt different. A desperate chill ran up my spine, and an instant headache materialized.

As the artificial turf dug into my arm, I did my best to move. I had to shake this off. Then, like a fool, I tried to shift my foot. My hands reached down and grabbed my right thigh, afraid if I went any lower I'd touch something I wouldn't want to. That thought and the excruciating pain caused a wave of nausea to flow through me. The last thing I wanted was to get sick on the field.

"Don't move, Trent. We need to stabilize you first."

I felt my thigh pads shift, and various hands on my body. Then I heard someone call for the medic. "I'm not going out in a cart. Help me up, I'll walk." It was then I noticed my teammates kneeling and the once raucous crowd's volume knocked down to murmurs. A couple of the coaches and medical staff hovered over me. "Slam it back into place."

I knew it was my patella. Once it was put back into place, I'd be fine. "We're taking you in for X-rays. Then we'll determine the course of action," our team's chief physician said. Thankfully, he was from the Rockets' staff so he knew me. And he knew I'd drag myself off this field before getting into a cart. That was until I tried to get into a sitting position and rather than seeing one of John, I saw four.

Still, I wanted to be upright when I left the stadium. "Help me up," I asked once more. Two of our coaches, who were former players, understood why I needed to do that, better than a doctor ever could. With one on either side of me, they squatted, adjusted my arms over their shoulders, and once I gave them the okay, they stood.

The sound of the crowd caused my eyes to shift around the field. My teammates and a couple others were still on one knee, others were standing and applauding. All except one. Beckett. I'd known him since high school. Even back then we were on rival teams. The fact that we just beat

Austin, which was who he played for, had me wondering if he was the one who hit me. Then he smirked, and I knew.

I'd be lying if I said I wanted to vomit right then and there. Thankfully the doctors had wrapped my leg so the fans wouldn't get an up-close view of my knee cap in an awkward position. When I set my left foot on the turf to help support myself, stars replaced my vision, and I knew the cart was in my future.

"Trent." Josh, one of the offensive line coaches, stopped moving. "You're too pale. I get it, but this isn't good, man. Let them take you."

If bile hadn't been perched at the base of my esophagus, I would have argued—instead, I nodded. Before I knew it, I was awkwardly sitting up on a flatbed, whistles blew, and the crowd noise amplified. There looked to be a scuffle in the distance, but between my pain and the cart being surrounded by coaches and staff, I couldn't see what happened.

Almost immediately the noise had been reduced to the sound of the cart's engine echoing in the tunnel. After I was gingerly moved from the cart and onto a bed in the medical room, everyone got to work. I went through the normal concussion protocols, and once completed, pain medication was administered. Thankfully, it didn't take long for it to kick in because before I knew it, I was in the back of an ambulance headed to the hospital.

Beeping, voices, and more beeping. "Can someone please turn that off?"

"There he is," Jackson's voice forced my eyes to open.

"Hey, what's going on?" Blinking a few times, I noticed his busted lip and black eye. I attempted to move, but my leg had been immobilized. "Why do you look like you were in an accident?" Pushing myself up, I grabbed the controller and waited for the head of the bed to raise me into a sitting position. That was when I noticed an IV in my left arm.

Suddenly, everything began rushing back. Moving the blanket aside, I saw the bandages and brace immobilizing my leg. I remember being carted off the field, in the back of an ambulance, signing paperwork, and lying in an MRI tube.

"No accident. How are you feeling? The doc just stepped out to go check on another patient. He should be back soon. Do you want anything? A nurse? The last one in here was very cute."

"I'm fine... what happened."

"Beckett happened. He got fined and will most likely be facing suspension."

"Had a feeling. And my leg?"

He rubbed the back of his neck, prompting me to stare at him. "Maybe you should wait for the doc."

Just then the door swung open and an older woman stepped in. "Glad to see you're awake, Mr. Archer. I'm Dr. Locke. How are you feeling?"

"Good, I suppose. And it's Trent. When can I leave?"

She smiled. "Well, that depends on a few things. First of all, I'd like to discuss your injury." A sudden bout of déjà vu flashed before my eyes as a lump slid down my throat and I silently prayed it wasn't serious. When I was injured in college, my doc told me I was lucky. Back then, I thought my world had ended. "You have a grade one tear of your posterior cruciate ligament… you may know it as your PCL." I did know it. It's the same thing that happened over five years ago. "You should be able to walk on it in about two to three weeks." *Okay, not horrible.* "Until then, you are to use crutches and not put any added stress on it outside of physical therapy."

"Got it. Anything else?"

"You also suffered a concussion. It was mild, but you need to make sure you follow the concussion protocols. I'm aware you know what they are, but I do have them for you as well."

"Okay, thank you."

"Do you have any other questions for me?" she asked, hugging her tablet to her chest.

"Just one, this isn't going to affect my career, right?"

"Trent, with any injury comes risk." She let out a calm breath, and I wasn't sure if it was for my benefit or hers. "You're a quarterback, correct?" When I nodded she went on to say, "Considering this is the second time you've injured your right PCL, and according to my records, you're right-side dominant, my recommendation would be no football for at least six to nine months."

I scoffed. "You're kidding, right? You just said, 'two to three weeks.'" I realized I sounded like an ungrateful jackass, but she had to be kidding. Nine months? Not a shot.

Unfazed by my small outburst she looked me square in the eyes. "Yes, two weeks before you can put pressure on it without the use of crutches. As I said, this is your second injury. The last thing I'm sure you want is any permanent damage."

A calendar popped up in my mind. Six months would bring us to August. I'd miss part of training camp and a bit of pre-season. Not too horrible, I suppose. Still, no offense to Dr. Locke, but her timeline seemed a bit excessive. Not wanting to argue or offend her any more than I probably already had, I simply countered with, "I'll talk to the team doctors."

"That's fine. They have been advised and will be evaluating your scans. Also…" *Great there's more.* "Along with your knee, and since you suffered a mild concussion, we'd like you to stay overnight and be reevaluated in the morning."

"Is that a recommendation or a requirement?"

She glanced at Jackson who shrugged.

"Recommendation." A beep followed by a man's voice came over the intercom asking for her to go to the nurse's station. "If you'll excuse me. Think about it, Trent. I'll be back as soon as I can. Dr. Scott, the orthopedic who read your chart and whose assessment I agree with will be back in the morning. Or as you said, you can talk to your team's doctors."

"Thanks, Doc."

She walked out and Jackson took a couple steps toward my bed. He pulled a phone out of his pocket that I recognized as mine. "You have a few texts and missed calls from Reese." Just hearing her name took the edge off. "Give her a call. I'm going to go grab a soda."

Before he walked out, I asked, "Hey, did we win?"

"Yeah. From what I understand, Booth knocked it through the uprights with two seconds left in regulation."

"From what you understand?"

His hearty laugh made me smile. "Yeah, I got ejected after I gave Beckett what he had coming to him. No one screws with my quarterback." Jackson smirked and walked out.

Smirking myself, I lifted my phone, and tapped the text icon. My mom's and Reese's were the only ones I decided to read. The others could wait. Most were reporters like Casey who probably wanted a scoop.

First went to my mother.

> *Hi. I'm fine. Please don't worry. I may be staying overnight in the hospital. I'll call you tomorrow.*

It took mere seconds for the bubbles to appear before her text chimed in.

> **Mom:** *Thank God. I was so worried. I heard on the news it could be serious.*

Of course reporters assumed the worst. All for ratings and clickbait.

> *I'll be fine in a couple of weeks. Talk soon, I promise.*

> **Mom:** *Okay, I love you. Don't give the doctors and nurses a hard time. They know what's best.*

The woman knew me well.

> *Yes, ma'am. Love you too.*

Rather than text Reese, I decided to call her. Thankfully, it only rang once.

"Hi. I've been so worried."

"You have?" When she didn't say anything, I realized how that must have sounded. "I mean, you didn't need to. I'm fine."

"You didn't look fine after that hit. And I heard you had a tear in your patella and concussion."

"*Partial* tear and *mild* concussion."

"Still awful. That lug, Beckett, got suspended. I hope he gets fined up the wazoo. I'm telling you if he was on the Thunder, I'd tell Granddad to kick him off the team."

Her feistiness had me genuinely feeling a bit lighter. "Miss Parker, if I didn't know differently, I'd think you really like me."

"I do really like you." She paused once more. Her voice taking on a more somber tone. "When I saw you hit the turf, it scared me. I've seen players get injured before but none that I was close to... personally."

Deciding I needed to see her and for her to see me, I clicked the video call icon. When she came into view, I grinned like a fool. No makeup, hair a bit disheveled, and it looked like she was in bed. When I glanced out the window, stars dotted the sky. Looking at the clock on my phone, it was after eleven p.m. Which meant after one a.m. in Virginia.

"You're a sight for sore eyes." Her eyes glassed over and it made me wonder if she was just tired or if she'd been upset. Hopefully, it wasn't the latter. "I didn't realize the time, did I wake you?"

She shook her head. "No, I couldn't sleep. I've been watching that play over and over again."

"I'm not sure I want to see it."

"Can't say that I blame you. Anyway, I was

thinking, why don't you stay with me while you recover? Unless, you have a nurse coming in."

I hadn't thought that far ahead. I've been hurt before and have managed. "You have no idea how I'd love for you to be my personal nurse, but staying with you under these conditions may be problematic... in... um... other areas."

Reese rolled her eyes. *God did I miss this girl.* "Fine. Then I'll come to your house." Not sure how that would be any different, but I let it go. "Are you sure you're okay?"

"Yes, I'm fine. Just might not be ice skating anytime soon."

"That's fine. We can binge watch television. I'll bring the cookies."

"Who has cookies?" Jackson walked in with my duffle bag in his hand. He strolled over to the head of the bed and looked at my phone. "Hey, Bird. Cute jammies."

I yanked my phone away and felt the IV cord tug. "Can you give us a second?" Jackson set down the bag, put his hands up as though he'd been busted robbing a bank, and walked out.

"When are you coming home?" Reese's yawn had been my cue to wrap up this call and let her get some rest. "Tomorrow. Since it's so late, I decided to stay here and appease everyone. I'll fly back as soon as I'm sprung."

"Okay. I'm really glad you're doing well, Trent.

When you get back and you feel up to it, I'd like to talk about us."

"Sweetheart, just hearing you refer to us as *us* is making me feel better by the second." Her pretty smile finally appeared. "Can I ask you something before I hang up?"

"Sure."

"Did you know Beckett was going to do that? I mean, did you notice it when he lined up."

She gave me a slight nod. "I had a feeling, yes."

"One day, you'll need to tell me your tricks."

"Usually, I keep that intel for Thunder players, but I suppose I can make an exception. It seems to be all I do when it comes to you anyway."

"Are you finally saying that I'm your exception?"

"Yeah, I guess I am."

"Good. Sleep well. I'll call you tomorrow."

I set the phone down and, although my heart filled with relief, my head still hurt. Dr. Locke walked in with Jackson. The pair stopped talking and looked at me.

"Doc, I'll be staying the night."

"Me too." Jackson pointed to the chair. "Team plane left already. I'll be flying with Trent tomorrow."

"Very well. I'll have the nurse bring you a pillow and blanket when she brings Trent's pain medication."

When the door closed behind her, Jackson waggled his brows. "Hope it's the cute one."

"You're such an idiot. Thanks for staying."

"Anything for my wingman. All good with the girlfriend?"

Not bothering to correct him, I simply grinned. "Yeah, everything is great."

Reese

WHEN I ARRIVED AT TRENT'S home, an exhausted looking Jackson answered the door.

"Hi, Bird. Wow, it's so good to see you."

He stepped aside and let me in. "Is the patient giving you trouble?" I asked, shrugging off my coat and hanging it along with my purse on the hooks next to the door.

Jackson laughed. "I've been staring at his ugly mug for over twenty-four hours."

"How is he?"

"Sleeping. I helped him up the stairs, but now that I think about it, he should have just slept on his recliner in the den, because I don't know how you're going to help him. No offense meant. I'm not saying you aren't strong—"

I put my hand up, cutting him off mid-sentence. "None taken. I'll just take him what he needs. No worries. Anything else I need to know?" We walked into Trent's kitchen, and that's when I noticed all of the flowers, balloons, and plants. "Wow."

"Yeah, that's the other thing, gifts have been pouring in. Fans, friends, family... including Alexa. She sent a box of cookies. They've stopped though, and he knows about all of them. Aside from that Lily, his housekeeper, was just here and stocked everything, so no worries about going to the store. Charlie, the team's doc, said he'll call Trent to set up a time for Kenny, he's one of the trainers, to come over. Trent had the guest house converted into a gym, so at least he won't need to leave here." I nodded, making a mental note of everything, but part of me thought I should be putting pen to paper.

Jackson was a great guy and friend. I could see why Trent liked hanging out with him. We exchanged numbers, and I walked him to the door. Before he left, he turned and smiled. "I'm glad he has you here."

"Funny, I just thought that of you."

"I like you, Reese Parker. I understand what he sees in you. The man is stubborn, you'll need patience." He gave me a wink before pulling the door closed behind him. Although Jackson was very easy on the eyes, I didn't get that feeling I had with Trent. No, when Trent looked at me, I felt it everywhere—my stomach would have that odd fluttery feeling, my skin would prickle, and my mouth would get dry. All of those things had never happened to me before. It was as though he had cast a magical spell on me.

Needing to see him with my own eyes, I took off my sneaks, and left them near the door. In socked feet, I quietly climbed the stairs, but once I got to the top, I had no idea which room was his. Glancing toward the left, I noticed a few doors, but something told me his would face the east where he could watch the sunrise.

One of the cherry wood floorboards creaked beneath my foot as I approached the last door in the hallway. When I pushed it open, I immediately spotted him asleep in the middle of what looked like a California king bed. Stepping inside, I slowly walked around to get the lay of the land, so to speak.

The creamy white walls were in contrast to his dark wood furniture. My finger trailed along his dresser as I looked at the framed pictures. One of him on a beach with an older couple he shared features with. He had the woman's smile and the man's stature. I could only assume they were his parents. In another one, he was with a bunch of guys from the team. And in one from draft day, Trent stood next to the league's commissioner, holding a Rockets' jersey with his name and the number two on the back.

I remember that day. How disappointed I felt for my granddad and the team. After I set the picture down, I glanced to my right and spotted a large, almost spa-like bathroom. It had the biggest shower I'd ever seen. When I moved closer, I realized it was more than a shower, it was a wet room complete with an egg-shaped tub at the end with multiple silver shower heads protruding from the walls. Raising my eyes, I noticed three more shower heads coming down from the ceiling.

The entire room was tiled with shiny smooth gray marble. Even most of the walls were tiled, if not fully, at least to the middle of them. White towels were neatly hung on hooks, the double sinks sat atop white marble just as exquisite as the flooring. It was a stunning room that rivaled any spa I'd ever been in.

After gawking and wondering what it would be like to slip into that tub after a long day, I moved back into the bedroom and slowly made my way to Trent. God, the man was stunning. His dark hair lay on his forehead, his lashes rested on his cheekbones, and his lips were a breath apart as he soundly slept.

Feeling a bit voyeuristic and not denying myself the opportunity to really study the man, my eyes traveled the length of his body. He must have shifted while I was in the bathroom because his sheet barely covered his abs... his very taut abs. His pecs looked smooth and solid with a light smattering of hair between them.

Continuing south, I noticed the bump in the covers, which I assumed was his brace. My heart broke a little for him. Knee injuries were awful for a normal person. For him, a star quarterback, they could be career ending. When I talked to my granddad about it, he merely stated it depended on the severity, and several other factors.

Not being able to resist, I lowered myself to the mattress, being careful not to bump his leg. As gently as I could, I brought my fingers to his forehead, pushed his wispy hair to the side, and kissed him. He shifted and cleared his throat. A smile tipped his lips, one eye opened, causing me to ask, "How long have you been awake?"

A snarky smirk blessed his face. "Only a few minutes. Thought I might be getting robbed. Then I saw this gorgeous girl and thought she could take whatever she wanted."

"You're funny."

"And you're a breath of fresh air."

"How are you feeling?"

"Careful, I may think you truly are beginning to care about me."

"Do you need me to say it again?" He nodded and his eyes slammed shut. Agony etched within the lines on his forehead. "Are you okay?"

"Yes, just a little pain."

I looked to the side to see his discharge instructions. "May I?" After he nodded, I scanned the first sheet. Thankfully the last time he'd received his pain medication had been notated. "You're due for your pills in about fifteen minutes. Can you manage until then?"

"Yeah, what else does it say?"

My eyes continued to roam the papers. "No weight on it for two weeks, use crutches..." I let my voice trail off reciting a few other restrictions. "Use a bag to cover the brace when showering or take a sponge bath while sitting." The thought of him naked in that glorious shower made my body tingle. Glancing up, his eyes were on me and his perfected smirk blossomed.

"I could go for a sponge bath. What do you say, want to be my nurse?"

When he winked, I abruptly stood, shifting the mattress. Trent's grimace made me feel bad. "I'm so sorry, I wasn't thinking. Are you okay?" He nodded. "I'm going to get you a glass of water so you can take your pills."

"Reese, I need to get up."

"Um... okay... why?"

"Because I need to pee."

I nervously laughed. "Right. Fine. Let me get your crutches." He pulled the covers back and an angry bruise that I hadn't noticed before marred the right side of his torso stopping me from moving. His naturally golden skin took on an angry purplish-blue hue tinged in yellow. "Oh my God. That looks horrible."

"Thankfully, it looks worse than it feels. If you could help me to the bathroom, I can take it from there."

"Okay." The rest of the covers fell away, and there was Trent in white boxer briefs and nothing else. Again, I found myself staring at him. In clothing, Trent Archer was gorgeous. In a football uniform, he was beyond sexy. However, boxer shorts that revealed just as much as a pair of women's lace panties, thrust him into a category I didn't have words for. What I did have was a bundle of nerves ready to turn me into a giddy fool.

"Reese?"

"Right, yes. How should we do this? I'm not that tall. How is this going to work? Maybe I should call Jackson or one of the team docs. Better yet—" I moved to the corner of the room and grabbed his crutches. "Here."

"You're adorable when you ramble," he teased.

"Whatever, I don't want you doing more damage. Just go about your business, and I'll grab your meds. Would you like anything else? A sandwich maybe? A cookie?"

"Lunch would be great. Whatever we have. Lily probably left some things in the fridge ready to go in the microwave."

Trent's arm muscles flexed as he slowly swung the crutches forward. When he stopped and looked at me, each muscle in his upper body was on pure display — rounded shoulders, biceps that resembled small mounds, triceps that were so defined, I could see each cut in them, and then there was his chest, abs, and those hip muscles that almost created an arrow right to his well-endowed manhood.

Who knows how long I stared at him, but when my observation didn't go unnoticed, embarrassment caused the blood to rush to my head. "If you need something, call me. I should only be a minute. I'll leave the door open."

The metal crutches clicked against the floor and as soon as he was out of sight, I scurried out of the room, down the stairs, and straight into the kitchen where I slammed back a glass of ice water. I then realized it would take much more than eight ounces of water to cool me off.

Happy that Lily had indeed left premade meals, I grabbed a submarine sandwich, a bag of chips from the pantry, a sports drink, and a cookie from the box Alexa had sent over. Placing them all on a bed tray Lily must have left out, I walked upstairs and when I was a step away from his door, the sound of metal hitting the wood floor startled me.

Rushing, I hurried through the doorway. Trent swore and bent down to reach his crutch that had fallen. I set the tray on the dresser and walked to the crutch before picking it up and handing it to him.

"Thanks, sorry, it slipped when I went to grab a T-shirt."

"I'll do it. I need you in bed."

"I never thought I'd hear you say those words." His chuckle was quickly replaced by a moan.

"Okay, funny man, where do you keep your shirts?"

"Second drawer on the left."

A few seconds later, Trent sat up in his bed, a bit more covered, eating his lunch, and thanks to the pain meds, feeling a bit better.

"I'm really sorry, Reese. My plan was to come back from Arizona, take you out, get to know you better, and for you to get to know me. This"—he waved his arm at his leg—"hadn't been in the plan. I should have listened to you." I didn't want to say *Yes, you should have,* so instead I reassured him that we had time to do more things.

"Thanks. Glad to hear that." Happy that he had an appetite, I let Trent finish his lunch and bottle of water in silence. Once done, he let out a breath. "I know you've done a lot already, but would you mind hanging out a bit longer?"

His eyes started closing. I grabbed the tray and set it on the floor beside the bed. "I have nowhere else to be."

Trent's whispered *thank you* was followed by

soft snores. I let out a yawn myself and for some reason, rather than moving to the cushioned chair in the corner, I scooched onto his mattress, and laid down next to him. His mattress was plush, soft, and the next thing I knew, my eyes slid closed, thankful that the man lying beside me was okay.

14

Trent

OUT OF HABIT, I SHIFTED my right leg only to be stopped by pain and the stabilizing brace. A grimace-filled growl rumbled out of me. The bed moved, and when I looked to my left, Reese was soundly sleeping next to me. Except she was on top of the covers rather than beneath them.

Why was she in my bed?

Why do I care?

Not wanting to wake her, and with my pain suddenly vanishing, I took time and studied her just as she had me earlier. Damn, she was gorgeous. The way her pretty lips separated as she took in soft breaths. Her lashes were gently resting just above her cheekbones while her hands formed a prayer position beneath her cheek.

Despite still being light outside, she must had been exhausted to fall asleep next to me. The urge to kiss her was overwhelming. As was my sudden urge to take care of business… so to speak. When I broke my gaze from her, I noticed my crutches weren't in reaching distance. They weren't clear across the room, so maybe I could make it to them on my own without waking Reese.

Slowly shifting the covers, I peeled them back, and once again angled my body.

"What are you doing?" Reese's motherly tone had me feeling as though I was back in high school and sneaking out for the night.

"I need to use the bathroom."

In a flash, she was out of bed, and moving toward my crutches. With both in one hand, she offered me her free one. "Here, I'll help you stand."

She pulled me up and when I stood our bodies were in perfect alignment. Well, as perfect as they could be considering I was about eight inches taller than she was, thanks to her sock-covered feet.

I rested my forearms on her shoulders, and my forehead on the top of her head. Breathing in the clean scent of what I guessed was her shampoo, which would most likely be on my pillowcase, I couldn't help but feel a sense of calm. That feeling was in total contrast to the thoughts in my head.

Ever since I ended up on the turf in agony, the fear of losing my career plagued me. It didn't matter how good of a season I had, or what a strong leader I'd been to the Rockets. What mattered to the organization was how good I'd be next season. In my opinion, physical therapy couldn't start soon enough.

"What's wrong?" Her sweet voice had me pulling her closer while doing my best not to set the foot of my right leg down.

"Just how much this sucks." Her hands that had been resting on my waist, slid back, and traveled up my spine as she held me close. "Thank you for being here."

Reese turned her head until her cheek was flat against my chest. "You're going to be okay. I know injuries are scary, but you're strong. I believe in you."

I leaned back and loosened my hold so I could look into her eyes. When our gazes met, I ran my thumb from her cheekbone to just under her bottom lip. Albeit awkward, my mouth met hers in a brief kiss. Knowing my banged-up body was in no position to take things further, getting either of us riled up wouldn't be the best idea. Between my occasional headache and the pain radiating from my knee, I'd need a week or two. Then, all bets were off.

She must have felt a similar emotion because she cleared her throat and reminded me that I got up for a reason. Chuckling, I released my hold on her, took the crutches she offered, and hobbled my way to the bathroom.

The entire process annoyed the hell out of me. I hadn't been out of my room all day, I hadn't watched any sporting news or even picked up my phone to check my social media. I flushed the toilet, leaned on the vanity, and stared into the mirror. The silver crutches resting against the wall were all I could see. Annoyed, I splashed some water on my face, brushed my teeth, turned to grab my crutches, and shuffled back to my bedroom.

Reese had fixed the covers, erasing any reminder that she had been in my bed. She leaned over and fluffed the spare pillow.

"Your bed felt like a cloud. It has to be the most comfortable mattress I've ever napped on. And I didn't intend to sleep, that says a lot right there."

"Have you been in many beds?" When her eyes sprung wide, I apologized. "Sorry, I'm not sure where that came from. Except that we don't know much about each other's pasts."

"Not to point out the obvious, but we have the time. I don't plan on going anywhere."

"Reese, as much as I love having you here, I don't want you to give up your social life. Plus, I'm tired of being in this room, and it's only been a day."

"Do you want to try and go downstairs? You may not be able to come back up though."

She giggled, and I glanced around my room. "That's fine. I'd rather be in my living room. Plus, I can manage the stairs."

Her brows furrowed. "Hmm… not sure that's a good idea. Jackson will probably come by tomorrow. I'd rather have him here to help."

I knew she was right, but sitting in bed with Reese near me was like putting a steak in front of a Tiger and telling him he couldn't taste it. Letting out a frustrated breath, I nodded and got back into bed.

"I'll go grab some food. It's just about dinner time. Any requests?" Steak was on the tip of my tongue, but I shook my head. A frown marred her face. "I'm really sorry that this happened to you. Your pain is okay right now though, right?"

"Yes, and I know you are. Thank you. As far as the pain pills, I'd rather switch to over the counter meds."

"Okay, whatever you'd like. But if it gets to be too much, we go back to your prescription."

"Deal."

Reese scurried out of the room, and as soon as I heard her hustle down the stairs, I slammed my arm into the pillow next to me and cursed. Rather than stare at my ceiling, I grabbed the remote off my side table and pressed a button. From across the room, my TV rose out of what looked like a normal credenza.

Turning it on and to the all-sports channel, I raised the volume and watched the college basketball game that was currently on. Better that than sports news and speculations about my career. An injured free-agent... what did that mean to my future? In an attempt to rid my head of that thought, I tossed the remote aside and watched West Virginia play Texas.

"Your wish has been answered." Reese glided in, sporting a bright smile.

When I looked up, Jackson stood behind her. "Bird told me you wanted to hang out downstairs. Plus, I was coming over anyway to check on you. I tried calling earlier, but this little lady never answered her phone."

I shook my head at his ridiculous nickname for Reese. And felt badly that my injury caused a disruption in my friend's life. That being said, I was happy to get out of this room.

"Sorry, my cell was on vibrate. I never heard it ring."

"It's fine, you're forgiven." Jackson slung his arm around Reese and kissed her temple.

A surge of jealousy burst in my chest. "Stop manhandling her and give me a hand instead, yeah?"

Jackson chuckled, winked at Reese who rolled her eyes at him, and finally brought me my crutches. "Let's go, lover boy."

Once again she giggled before walking out of my room. I clicked off the television and with painstakingly slow steps made my way down the stairs where I was surprised to see Alexa in my kitchen.

She turned and her smile vanished. *God, how pitiful did I look?* "Hey, Trent. How are you feeling?"

Jackson handed me my crutches, and I used them to make my way toward the kitchen island. "Hi. I'm feeling as good as can be expected. Could be worse." Alexa nodded and glanced to Reese, who gave her a weak smile. "All right, let's get something straight." My voice raised enough for the trio to look at me.

"I know that this just happened, and I know that you all feel badly about it. As much as I appreciate your concern, I'm fine, really. My leg will get stronger every day, especially after I start physical therapy. Injuries go with the territory. It's not the first time and won't be the last."

"I'm sorry. This is all new to me." Alexa's worrisome tone made me feel terrible for raising my voice. Then she lifted a white bakery box. "I brought cookies because in my opinion they're way better than chicken soup. Not that you're sick, but you know when you're down and out. Not that you're —"

I raised my hand and chuckled. "I get it, and thank you."

Jackson clapped his hands together. "Okay, now that we have all of that cleared up, the pizza that I brought is going to get cold. Can we eat please? I'm starving."

"You just had five cookies," Alexa scolded.

"Takes more than a few cookies to satisfy me."

Alexa turned red and that seemed to have Reese, who had been quiet for the past few minutes step in. "I'll get the plates. Trent, would you like to eat here or would your recliner be better?"

Once it was settled that we'd eat in my family room, I sat in my favorite chair with my leg up, Reese and Alexa sat on the couch, and Jackson made himself comfortable in the chair across from mine. Despite the fact that I'd rather be staring at Reese, it was nice to have them all here.

Reese

ALONE ONCE AGAIN, TRENT AND I sat in his family room. Thanks to my earlier nap, I wasn't the least bit tired, and by the way the patient fidgeted, neither was he.

"Can I get you anything?"

"No. I don't want you waiting on me," he grumbled.

"Sorry, but I hate to state the obvious…"

"Yes, I know. I'm sorry. I didn't mean to snap at you. Truly. It's just, I'm not used to being taken care of. My next house is going to be a ranch."

I couldn't help but laugh. "How about we watch some TV?" He nodded, I grabbed the remote and pressed the power button. Naturally, the sports network was on. Not knowing if he'd be one of the stories, or if they'd show the hit that landed him in this predicament, I changed the channel. "Any requests?"

"Whatever you'd like."

Testing that theory, I put on the channel that played cheesy romance movies. I shouldn't even say cheesy, because there had been days when I stayed in my pajamas all day and watched a marathon of love stories.

The movie had just started, and about thirty minutes in the couple's first date had just ended. After the commercial break and Trent complaining about the feminine product ads, a scene started where the leading couple stood on the porch of an old white house. He looked her in the eyes while holding both her hands in his. *"Thank you for a great night,"* she said. *"Call me tomorrow?"*

The tall man, smiled, kissed her cheek, and walked away. The scene dissolved with her walking into her house.

"What a pansy," Trent said, making me giggle. "Maybe he should use some of those products we just saw."

My mouth gaped, and I did my best not to encourage him with the laugh that sat on the tip of my tongue. "Why do you say that? He was being a gentleman."

"The dude blew it. Nope, they're not going to last."

I knew they were going to last because they were the main characters. Although, I did watch a movie once where they ended up as friends and not in a relationship. Then I looked at Trent. Could that happen to us if our lives were a movie? I could see being his friend now that I knew him a little better… even if my lady parts decided to wake up and virtually wave at the man every time he was in the room. At one point last night, they smacked me, probably wondering why I was making them wait.

"You don't know that they won't make it. What would you have done differently? Seduced her?"

"Yes, Reese. That's exactly what I would have done. Right there on that wooden porch, for all the neighbors to see, I would have slid her jacket off her shoulders and let it fall. Then I would have teased the swell of her breasts with my fingertips, while softly peppering her neck with my lips. All the while, her sweet perfume would be making it harder for me to stand still.

"Then, I'd drag my fingers into her hair, tip her head back, and kiss her as though I needed her air to breathe. Then she'd invite me in, and I'd bring her to such immeasurable pleasure that no other lover would ever compare. The next scene would be me leaving in the morning with a bounce in my step." All I could do was blink. "See, my way is better right?"

Not wanting to relent or admit that I could feel my heart race a bit faster, feel his fingers in my hair, or the way my skin prickled when he mentioned kissing her neck, I merely shrugged. "If you say so."

He chuckled. "Don't quit your day job. Acting is not your forte."

"Ha ha." Trent stared at me a moment. His pretty eyes locked onto mine and if I hadn't looked away quickly, I might have asked him to play out that scene he'd just described. "What's that look for?"

"I'm just wondering if things would have been different between us if we would have met under different circumstances. Don't get me wrong, I'm loving every minute of this, but what are we going to tell our kids and grandkids?" Blinking, because that was clearly all I'd been capable of when he said something to throw me off balance, I didn't say anything. *Kids? Grandkids? What?!* "I met your mom because she gave me the finger in front of millions of people," he went on to say as if talking to our invisible children.

I shook my head. "You're ridiculous."

"They won't think so once I show them the photographic proof of that meme."

"No, I mean you're ridiculous saying we're going to end up together and have kids."

Dreamy music coming from the television had him pointing in that direction. "Look, if Mr. Massengill can get a woman, there's hope for us."

"Oh my God, I can't believe you just said that." He shrugged, and the laugh I'd been suppressing couldn't be reined in any longer. It flew from my mouth and a sudden case of the giggles hit me full force. Maybe I was tired, but when I glanced up and Trent seemed to be staring at the television, the giggles rolled on and on.

Catching my breath and dabbing the tears from my eyes, I regained some of the composure I'd lost. "If you want to change it, you can."

Trent shook his head. "No way. I'm invested now. Let's face it, she's a total babe." I glanced at the screen, and she was a gorgeous woman. Tall, curvy, dark eyes, heart-shaped face, and dark hair that rested just above her shoulders. "Although, I prefer blondes."

When I looked at him, his eyes were no longer on the television but on me. "Tell me we have a chance, Reese. I know you said I was your exception, but humor me and say the words."

Maybe the hit he took had him needing reassurance. There had been no doubt in my mind he'd be asking the same of his physical therapist. Knowing Trent, he'd want to be practicing the day his therapy ended. If it took me to help him emotionally, how could I deny him that? Especially when it had been the truth.

"We have a chance, Trent. I told you, I don't date players… on or off the field. You're different, I guess. Not at all what I thought."

"Thanks, Reese. You're exactly what I thought you were."

"What do you mean?"

"The first time I saw you in the stands. I thought that woman is gorgeous, feisty, and confident. A couple other descriptions may have run through my mind, but that's not the point. What *is* the point is, I like you, a lot. Thank you for being here."

Emotion began to swell, shooting a tingle up into my face, behind my nose and eyes. His smile caused mine. "I wouldn't want to be anywhere else."

Swoony music came on once again, and when we looked at the TV, the couple's lips were fused together in a shockingly steamy kiss. "There you go, Mr. M! I knew you had it in you."

That time, I couldn't stop from bursting out into laughter. "You're ridiculous."

Before we knew it, the credits started to roll. "Want to watch another one?" he asked, looking comfortable.

"I'll get the popcorn."

Thanks to Trent's profession, his physical therapy would take place in his at-home gym that rivaled those requiring a monthly fee. It didn't just have a treadmill and a few free weights. This room spanned the back of his house and included every Nautilus machine I'd ever used. The area was bigger than the first floor of my house and filled with weights and a couple benches, a basketball court, and of course, a steam room and sauna. If this were mine, aside from grocery shopping, I didn't think I'd ever leave my house... maybe not even then.

After our movie marathon, Trent assured me he'd be okay. I left him with everything he needed. Thanks to his motion recliner, I didn't worry too much. Plus, despite him wanting me to play nurse, I knew a lot about athletes. They were strong physically, but their egos outweighed their strength by leaps and bounds. Having me there, negated both of those. So, I slept at home.

Knowing the physical therapist employed by the Rockets was due there at any moment, I sent him a quick text.

> *Good morning. How are you feeling?*

> **Trent:** *Good. Better. Kenny should be here soon. I just want this damn brace off.*

> *I know. Be patient.*

> **Trent:** *That's not one of my virtues.*

I laughed before typing back,

> *You have virtues?*

> **Trent:** *You're funny in the morning. I did miss seeing you when I woke up. Will you be coming over later?*

Jackson had messaged me to let me know a bunch of the guys were heading to Trent's place later on, and wondered if I would mind. That comment threw me off kilter. Why would I mind? I didn't live there.

> *I don't thinks so. Jackson and a few of the guys will though.*

> **Trent:** *I know. But you're prettier than my teammates. Well, maybe not Troy because he is a cutie.*

He paused for a moment and just as I was ready to text him back, tiny dots danced before his message appeared.

> **Trent:** *Nah. Never mind, you're prettier.*

> *Are you back to taking your pain pills?*

> **Trent:** *LOL No. Just in a better mood. Kenny just got here. I'll talk to you later.*

> *Ok. Don't push yourself.*

He sent me a thumbs-up emoji, and I got out of my car and walked into the bakery. The smell of sugar and coffee hit me like a slap to the face — which was what I needed because my body had just realized my sleep schedule was messed up.

"Good morning, Reese," Erica said, putting a tray of moon shaped cookies into the case. "You look tired. Would you like some coffee?"

"Hi. Yes, you know me so well." I plucked a pink apron off the hook behind the counter and slid it on. "Sorry I haven't been here." She handed me a cup of caffeine, and I couldn't help but bring it to my nose and inhale before taking a sip. "So good."

"Come sit. We have a few minutes before we open. How's Trent feeling? Alexa told me what happened. So violent."

I nodded. I knew what she meant. Football could be violent if not played with the reverence it deserved and was expected of professional athletes. Beckett defied all of that when he put that hit on Trent. No better than a mobster who shot his enemy.

"He's doing better. His physical therapist is there now."

All I could do was pray it all went well. That the injury he suffered wouldn't be career-ending. Trent definitely didn't think so since he didn't completely tear his ligaments, but it had been the second time it happened. I knew enough about the sport to know that things turned on a dime no matter how good you were. The fact that Kenny worked for the Rockets' organization meant he'd be a direct line to the coaching staff, who in turn would be the line to the GM. From there, who knows what would happen.

"Reese, where'd you drift off to?"

I soothed Erica's concerned look with a smile and lame explanation. "Sorry, it's been a long few days."

"Maybe you should go home and rest."

"No, but thank you. I miss being here."

The door chimed and Alexa walked in. "Good morning! Isn't it a glorious day?"

Her mother and I looked at one another. I knew Erica thought her daughter was in a good mood, but something told me it was more than that. When I cocked a brow, she winked. Yes, definitely more than that.

At least one of us was having sex. Not that Trent wouldn't have found a way if I'd given him any indication that I was ready to take our relationship in that direction, but sex meant more to me than the physical act. No, I didn't need to be in love, but I wasn't one to roll in the sheets just for fun either.

Even in college, I didn't sleep around. I had a short relationship with someone I met in Europe. He was Parisian and stunning. His accent had been enough to send me over the edge. We had met on a museum tour. After a month of seeing one another every day, we had sex. In my head, I imagined moving to France and living on croissants and *croque monsieur*. Except, I lived here, he lived there, neither wanted to move, so he was now in my memories of a very sweet time in my life — literally and figuratively.

I wasn't sure where things would go with Trent, but the heat in his eyes and the way he described what he would do if he were in that movie, had me wishing I was his co-star. Oh boy, I had it bad for Trent Archer.

16

Trent

S WEAT DRIPPED FROM MY TEMPLE, behind my ear, and down my neck until it landed on the padded bench I'd been lying on. Kenny was one of the top trainers, and knowing that, I gritted my teeth and did my best not to wince as he manipulated my leg and hip.

"Doing okay, kid?"

"Yeah," I grunted, feeling anything but okay.

I'd been through this before, but this time it felt a bit different. Either that, or I blocked out the pain I felt five years ago. However, back then, I was younger and less beat up. In my profession, it didn't matter that I was still shy of my twenty-ninth birthday, my body felt older. That being said, my career was far from seeing its end.

"We'll move to electrodes and start some contractions. I looked at your films the hospital sent over and compared them to your old ones. What concerns me is you've injured the same knee twice now."

"What are you getting at?"

Maybe it was the cold stare I had on him or my clipped tone, but Kenny held his hands up. "Look, my job is to make sure the players are healthy. If I need to spell it out for you, this is your planting leg. You push off on this leg." I nodded because he only said what I already knew. "My *job*, like I said, is to make sure you're healthy without doing any more damage to your knee. And, of course, ensure the team has all the necessary information to make any decisions they need to. Much like the doctor in the hospital gave to you. Everyone wants what's best for you."

All I could do was blink while my blood pumped heavily through my veins. "Then we should get to work, so I'm ready for the season." I gave him a tight grin and after his single nod, he continued to stick probes on my leg surrounding my knee and a couple on my thigh.

"Lean back, I'm going to go grab some ice." I nodded. "And Trent," he said before walking away, "I'm not the enemy here."

"I know. I'm just frustrated. Sorry for acting like a jackass." The last thing I wanted was to throw a pity party for myself. It wasn't warranted and definitely wasn't my style.

"Apology accepted."

Kenny disappeared from my sight, and the fact that he didn't negate the personality assessment I gave myself, made me feel worse than I already did. I rested my arm on my forehead and took a few deep breaths. There was zero doubt in my head that I would be strong enough. All I needed to do was listen to Kenny, do my exercises, and not push myself.

For the next thirty minutes and even after Kenny left, I stayed in my gym and worked out my left leg. All I could think about was what he said about planting my foot. I wasn't ambidextrous by any stretch of the imagination, but I'd make sure both of my legs were stronger than ever. At a sound I glanced toward the door.

"Hey," Jackson said, ambling toward me with a bottle of water in his hand. "Figured you'd still be in here." When I raised a brow, he answered my silent question. "Kenny let me in. All okay?"

"Great," I clipped before inhaling and releasing a frustrated breath. "Sorry. This just sucks is all."

"Yeah, I know. Do what Kenny says, and you'll be fine. Anyway, what else do you have going on today?"

What could I have going on? "Nothing. Going to try and shower, then I don't know. I'm tired of sitting on my butt all day. Despite how nice my walls are, I'm sick of staring at them."

"Then, let's get out of here. Feel like grabbing a bite to eat? Sounds like a change of scenery may do your ornery ass good."

"Definitely." I leaned over, grabbed my crutches, and followed Jackson out of the gym. And as soon as I got into my room, I slid on the plastic bag Kenny gave me that would cover my brace and worked my way into the shower.

Letting the hot water rinse away my morning, I began to feel a bit better. Deep down, I knew I'd be fine. Could be worse, this could have happened during pre-season, and then the regular season would have been messed up. Bracing my hand against the cool marble, I let the water beat down on the back of my neck and shoulders.

An image of Reese's smile popped into my head, and rather than stand there any longer, or turn the dial to cold, I got out, dried off, and asked Jackson if he was in the mood for a cookie.

"Do all athletes eat this much sugar?" Alexa asked Jackson, who just ordered two dozen snickerdoodles.

"Some of us are naturally sweet," I added with a laugh. "Is Reese around?"

"Not right now; she had a meeting with her

grandfather this morning. She said she had to read the report the scouts wrote." Alexa shrugged. "No clue what that means. Then she mentioned the draft… I think."

Jackson and I just looked at her. Then my tight end decided to voice our mutual thoughts out loud. "Scouting reports about the college draft?"

"Yes!" She snapped her fingers in the air. "That's it. Still don't understand it, but yes. That's what she is doing. Anyway, she should be in at some point, just don't know when exactly."

A group of guys who looked to be high school age strolled in and stopped dead in their tracks when their focus went to Jackson and me. One had on a Thunder cap, one a high school emblem, and the others were Rockets fans.

When neither of us said anything, I glanced over at Alexa, who shrugged. It was refreshing in a way that she had zero clue who we were or what our profession meant to this town. Nor did she seem to care. Just then, Reese walked in and when she saw the stand-off, she shook her head and smiled.

"Okay, boys, step aside or order something because you're blocking the counter." Reese made a couple of them jump with her sudden teacherly tone—an image of her dressed as a hot teacher popped into my head. Remembering where we were, I quickly tossed that aside and promised myself I'd save it for later.

The kids' eyes flicked between Reese and me. "It's you!" the guy wearing the Thunder hat said. "You're my hero," he gushed, looking at her rather than Jackson or me. Reese's brows furrowed. Then the kid held up his phone. His screensaver was a picture of Reese flipping me off. When Reese's lips curled between her teeth, I knew she was repressing a smile. "I wrote a paper on your grandfather for my sports management class. You're so lucky to know him. I can't imagine what that would be like. Don't get me wrong," he continued to ramble, "I love my granddad, but he's an accountant. Great guy, but you get to work with a legend in the best sport ever." His buddy nudged him. "I'm Graham Easton. Totally stoked right now."

He held out his hand, which Reese took in hers. "It's a pleasure to meet you. I'm Reese Parker."

The kid nodded, looking as though he just met his idol. It was a look I knew well. *Good for her, I thought.*

"Graham applied for a summer internship with the Thunder," that same friend added with another nudge.

Graham flicked his yes at him before nodding. "Second year in a row. It's a tough gig to get."

Reese appraised him before asking, "What is it you want to study in college?"

"Economics. I want to be a GM for a pro team one day. I recently was accepted into Sutton's Business School."

"That's a great goal and school." The pride of being an alum of that same school had been evident—to me at least. "How about this, why don't you email me, and I'll have personnel pull your file. I can't guarantee anything, but I'll put in a good word for you. After all, you are going to my alma mater. Trent's too."

His friends all clapped him on his back and jostled him around. "It's a great school. Thanks so much, Ms. Parker."

"My pleasure."

After the love fest for Reese ended, the guys stood at our table. We chatted for a while, signed a couple autographs, and took some pictures.

"Sorry about your knee," one kid said to me. "Beckett sucks." Not bothering to disagree—because I didn't—I merely nodded. "It's because you beat him. Can't wait until next year."

Neither can I. Never ever would I wish bodily harm on anyone, but when we played against Beckett again, I wanted to run up the score. Plays had already formulated in my head. I began to write them down when I couldn't sleep, and the next time I saw the offensive coordinator, I'd talk to him about it.

As much as it stunk being laid up, it gave me time to plan a couple strategies that would throw defenses off guard. My instinct was to run them by Reese because she had a diabolically analytical brain, but then I needed to remember that we weren't on the same team… professionally. Personally, though, a completely different story.

I glanced up, and Reese was laughing with Alexa behind the glass case. She must have sensed my eyes on her, because when she turned her head, a pretty rosy hue filled her cheeks. A second later Alexa said something, and our connection was broken. That was until she turned around and winked before sliding a pink apron on.

Then an image of her in that apron… and *just that apron* flew into my head. Man, I had it bad. Moving my attention to Jackson, he just shook his head. "Dude, you're staring."

"Yeah, I know. Can you blame me?"

Jackson looked at the two friends who were looking back at us. "Not one bit," he said.

Yeah, I couldn't agree more. Snagging my crutches, I abandoned Jackson and made my way toward the door that said employees only. When Reese noticed me, she furrowed her brows, and walked to where I stood.

"Everything okay?" she asked, concern lacing her sweet voice. I hated that was the first thing I heard anytime I spoke to someone. I understood the reason behind the question, it just got old quickly.

"Yes, I just need a minute, can I…?" I tilted my head toward the door.

"Oh, of course." She gingerly moved past me,

opened the door, and I followed her inside. A small table with two chairs, a water cooler, and a door with a restroom plaque on it was off to the right. The only thing missing since the last time I'd been in this room was Bubba. She pulled out a chair, but I waved her off. "Is it your leg? You had PT today, right?"

"Yeah, but it's not my leg."

Her brows furrowed before she nodded. "Those guys talking about the game?"

"No, it's not the guys."

"Then what's wrong?"

"I wanted to be alone with you." Adjusting the crutch under my right arm, I released the grip, and cupped her face. Reese blinked, and I maneuvered myself closer to her. Her breaths deepened, forcing her chest to rise and fall with measured movements.

Wanting to take my time, but failing miserably, I gently pulled her forward until our lips were a fraction apart. Only the stale air in the room passed between them. While my eyes remained open, hers were closed. I could see movement behind her lids, and before she thought twice about kissing me at work, I leaned forward and closed the space between us.

Her hands were on my hips. Her scent of some sort of sweet citrus, filled my nostrils, and all I could do was take it all in. While my lips fused to her soft feminine ones. Everything about this woman turned me on. I could feel my body come to life, and in a few seconds so would she if I didn't pull away. Not exactly appropriate for where we were. If we were anywhere else, and if I didn't feel as though my knee was on fire, I would have been able to show her exactly how much she meant to me.

When I broke our connection, she opened her eyes, and those pretty lips of hers curved up. "Will you come over later?"

"Sure."

I slid my index finger under the strap of her apron that went around her neck. "Will you wear this?" When her brows drew together, I added, "*Just* this?"

She swatted my arm. "You're ridiculous."

"And you're gorgeous. One day, Miss Parker. One day, I'm going to have you in my bed, all to myself. When that day comes, the only thing you'll be wearing is that pretty smile of yours."

"Is that so?" she teased, crossing her arms in front of her chest.

"It's most definitely so."

Jackson knocked on the door before sliding inside. "Word got out that we're here. The place is jammed."

On a normal day and when I didn't feel as though there was a hot poker lodged in my knee,

I'd be all for meeting the fans, but today wasn't a normal one. "Can we use the back door?"

Reese nodded. As soon as we stepped into the small hallway the buzz and murmurs from the front of the store filled the air. "I need to go help them," Reese said. "You know where it is, Trent. The alarm isn't on so you can go right out."

"I'll grab the car and pull it around back," Jackson said before hustling toward the door.

I looked at Reese. "Thank you. I'll see you later?"

"Sounds good." She graced me with one more gorgeous smile before walking away.

"Hey, Reese?" I called out. Her blonde hair whipped around when she faced me. "Don't forget your apron."

She rolled her eyes and laughed. At least she didn't give me the finger. Progress. I chuckled and hobbled my way outside.

Reese

IT HAD BEEN TWO WEEKS since Trent's injury and thankfully, he seemed to be getting stronger. I sat in his room as he showered. Looking around, I decided to straighten up a bit. Granted, thanks to Lily, it wasn't a mess, but there were a few drawers that needed to be closed, a sock or three that had seemed to have missed the hamper's opening, and a couple empty water bottles on his bedside table.

Once the dresser and hamper were situated, I gathered the water bottles and saw the discharge papers. Wondering if there was anything special he should be doing two-weeks into the injury, and knowing that he had given me permission to read the information, I flipped the page to the assessment section.

My eyes scanned what I already knew. An instant

smile spread across my face when I realized he'd be able to ditch the crutches soon. Not so much for me, but for him. I knew Trent disliked them. One thing about the man, even depending on two metal walking assistants annoyed him.

There was a section about concussions, which reminded me that I needed to ask him if he had been getting headaches. Then my heart slammed into my ribcage. The doctor at the hospital told him he couldn't play football for six to nine months? Trent hadn't mentioned that to me. I glanced at the bathroom door suddenly feeling as though I had invaded his privacy.

Setting the papers down, I plopped onto the edge of the bed, ignoring the empty bottles toppling to the floor. I didn't know how many minutes had passed, but when the door opened, Trent stood there, bare chested, towel hanging low around his waist, wearing a gold necklace I never noticed before, and his hair damp, making him look sexier than normal.

Not saying a word, my gaze trespassed all over his body, enjoying the view, but when it landed on his knee, I remembered what I'd just read.

"Hey, everything okay? You have a weird look on your face." He tucked the crutches under his arms and swung them my way. Trent glanced down and with his right crutch, pointed to the empty water bottles. "Reese?"

"Sorry." I leaned down and picked up the

bottles, setting them on the table where they had been. Of course that packet grew lips and told me to come clean, which I did. "I… why didn't you tell me your doctor said you couldn't play ball for six to nine months?"

Trent's face reddened, his skin sprouted goose bumps, and I knew it hadn't been because it was still a tad damp. "She isn't my doctor and doesn't get the privilege to assess me. That is why the Rockets have a medical staff. They know what's best for me. Not a doctor who has known me for a minute. I'm not saying she isn't qualified, I'm sure she is very good at her job, but her assessment is wrong."

I'd never heard the smug tone in his voice before. "Okay, what did your therapist say?"

"That I'm getting stronger. I can ditch these things"—he nudged his crutches forward—"in a couple of days. Everything is on schedule. Maybe I'll send Dr. Locke tickets to opening day."

"I'm sorry, I didn't mean to upset you."

His head dropped forward. When he looked up, those wispy hairs laid haphazardly on his forehead. "No, I'm sorry. I sound like a jerk. It's just… she's wrong. I'll be fine."

All I could do was agree with him. First, I was the furthest thing from a medical professional. Second, I knew the tenacity players had. They weren't immortal, but they were definitely stronger than the average Joe. I took a step forward and could feel the heat radiating off him.

The scent of his soap surrounded me and now it was my skin that prickled.

"No, apologies. I'm the one who's sorry." My focus landed on his necklace and the charm that hung from it. A pattern was embossed in the center, but I didn't know what it was.

Trent must have read my mind. "It's the path of life. When I left for the pros, my mom got it for me. It was very difficult for me to leave her. She was in remission, but it terrified me that the cancer could come back and do a worse toll on her. At the same time, she felt badly that I didn't want to go to DC any longer."

"You didn't?"

"Not really. I wanted to be closer to her. It was something I struggled with. The day I needed to give my answer, was the day she gave me this." He fingered the charm between his finger and thumb. "She said it was a reminder that even though she wasn't with me physically, I wasn't alone. She was with me." He shook his head. "Not going to lie, it freaked me out a bit. Almost sounded ominous when she had meant it to be the opposite. Anyway, when we played in San Diego, the clasp broke. I was at her house, she insisted I get it fixed. I just got it back."

Tears filled my eyes hearing the story. And for some strange reason unbeknownst to me, I leaned forward and kissed his charm, letting my lips graze his chest. Leaning back, I tilted my head and smiled at him. "That's really beautiful."

"Yes, it is."

Our eyes locked, and after regaining my composure, I asked, "What do you want to do today?"

He waggled his brows and despite feeling desperately turned on by the Adonis in front of me, I shook my head. "Fine," he conceded. "Let me get dressed, and I suppose we can watch a movie."

"A sappy one?"

"Is there any other kind?" I laughed, happy that Trent's sarcasm had returned. Either that or he was growing to like romance movies. Whichever one it was, I'd take it. Spending this much time with him had become something I looked forward to. "What's that look for?"

Shaking my head, I couldn't come up with an answer that made any sense. Then again, opting for the truth had always been my go-to. "I'm just wondering how I could have been so wrong." A sudden wave of sadness and disappointment in myself settled in my heart.

He kissed the top of my head. "You can make it up to me when I'm healed." I returned his salacious grin with one of my own. "Now, let's get out of this room before I toss these crutches and throw you onto the bed."

An image of the two of us popped in my head. If I were a selfish person who didn't care about the ramifications to his injury, I would have taken him up on that offer. But for now, the visual and promise of things to come would need to suffice.

"Okay, let's go. We wouldn't want to miss the start of our movie marathon."

Trent chuckled. "Nope. Wouldn't want to miss that."

We made our way down the stairs, something that Trent had quickly mastered. I knew for sure that if I had an immobilizing brace on, I'd have a hard enough time walking, let alone navigate eighteen steps.

We took our respective places on the sofa and flicked the television on. After about two hours, and before the second movie started, I went into the kitchen, made a quick dinner, brought it back to the family room, and handed Trent his plate.

"Thanks, this looks great." He lifted his steak and cheese sandwich and took a generous bite. "Wow, so good."

I nodded. "It's one of my granddad's favorites. Speaking of which, when I was at his office the other day, he invited us both over for dinner when you're feeling up to it. I meant to tell you at the bakery when I saw you, but the frenzy of fans ensued, and I forgot."

"I'd love to have dinner with your grandparents. What does he think of us?"

Before answering, I took a sip of my water. I

hadn't really said much to Granddad about Trent and me. Just that we were getting to know one another and were friends. Going for lighthearted, I lifted my sandwich and before taking a bite, I nonchalantly said, "He knows I no longer want to slap you, if that's what you mean."

"Another bonus. So he doesn't know that when I look at his granddaughter all I want to do is kiss her, strip her down, and make love to her until she becomes a Rocket—" he winked, giving the word a new meaning in my brain—"fan."

All I could do was chew and stare. No, that wasn't all I did. My dumb eyes wandered down to the basketball shorts he was wearing. When he chuckled, I finally spoke. "I definitely don't think you should say any of those things."

The laughing ceased and those gorgeous eyes of his met mine. "Even if I mean them?"

"Especially if you mean them."

"Noted. All sex aside, I would like to go if you'd like me to."

I nodded. "At least we won't need to travel far, so that's a bonus."

Imagining Trent sharing a meal with my family didn't seem to scare me. I'd never really taken a boy, or in his case man, to meet my grandparents. Aside from a casual date who had to come to the house when I was a teenager, Trent would be the first one. And for some reason, I was happy about that.

18
Trent

EVERY DAY SINCE MY INJURY seemed to blend together. On the bright side, each day my leg felt stronger and I started to feel more like myself. And better still, Reese and I had gotten closer. We sat on my couch munching on kettle corn when the gate's buzzer sounded.

"It's probably Jackson," I said to Reese as I picked up my phone to connect with the app linked to the gate. Tapping the screen, a delivery van came into view. "Yeah, can I help you?"

Thanks to my profession and popularity, some good and some not, I didn't buzz everyone in just because a business's name was slapped on the side of their vehicle. Plus, it was a bit late for a delivery.

"Hi," a young voice said. "I'm so sorry, but I couldn't find your house. I have a delivery for you from Dina's Florist." She must have sensed my hesitation because I watched her shift around in her seat before lifting her hand presenting her ID to the camera perched on the speaker. "I'm Emily, Dina's niece. You can call her if you'd like to."

Despite her not being able to see me, I smiled. "It's all good. Thank you." Tapping the screen once more to allow the gates to open, I said, "Come on up."

She thanked me and Reese stood. "I'll get it. Stay here." I watched as she grabbed money from her purse before heading to the door. When the doorbell rang, two voices filtered in and silenced as soon as Reese closed the door.

A large bouquet of red roses mixed with other varieties I didn't know the names of blocked Reese's face. She set them down, plucked the card out of the plastic fork-like holder, and handed it to me.

Sliding the note out of the envelope, I scanned the message, and noticed it was from Casey McGrath. *Fantastic.*

Trent,

I hope you're feeling better. If there is anything I can do, please let me know. I'd be more than happy to be your private nurse. Call me.

Casey

I glanced over at Reese, who resumed her spot on the couch, thankful she had her attention back to the television. When I looked at the screen and saw a commercial for fabric softener was on, I knew she was purposely diverting her focus. Either that or she found the fact that a toy could bounce on towels while smelling like baby powder riveting.

I immediately felt as though I had two choices: one, tell Reese who the flowers were from; two, toss the card aside and play it off as though they were from a fan. Except, not only was the beautiful woman smarter than that, she also deserved the truth.

"They're from Casey McGrath." With the card between my fingers, I stretched my arm out to hand it to her.

She slowly looked at me, then to my offering; those beautiful eyes of hers held me captive. "I don't need to read it. Believe me, the woman didn't hide how much she likes you." I cocked a brow. "During your sideline interview at the game. Both Alexa and I noticed the familiarity between you two."

"Ah, yes. That."

"Yes, that." Reese smiled. "It's okay. I know you two had a fling for a while. It's hard not to make headlines when the golden boy dates the pageant queen."

"We didn't actually date, so to speak. We more

or less went on dates." Reese laughed and shook her head. "Okay, that sounded dumb. What I meant was, we weren't in a relationship. We'd go to events from time to time."

"And sleep together." Her eyes widened. "I'm sorry, that's none of my business. You don't need to respond."

My heart jumped into my throat. This was all uncharted water to me. Did I just come clean and tell her? Did I need to? Would I want to know if the tables were reversed? No. Just thinking about another man's hands on Reese made me see all sorts of red. But, I had no right since we weren't defined.

Despite all of that, I told her the truth. "Yes, you're right. We had a physical relationship. I'm not even going to say with you it's different because you already know that it is. Casey and I haven't been together in months."

"It's fine, Trent, really."

Like a man possessed, I grabbed my phone off the sofa's arm, clicked open my contacts, and pulled up Casey's number. Of course she answered on one ring, and practically purred the word, "Hello."

"Hi, Casey, it's Trent." I slid my eyes to Reese who watched me from the corner of hers. "Thank you for the flowers. They're very nice. I thought you should know that I'm in a relationship." The corner of my lips quirked up when Reese's eyebrows shot to her hairline.

"Hey, Trent. Oh, I'm sorry, I didn't know. Off the record, can I assume it's with Reese Parker? I heard you two were getting very friendly."

"Right now, we're keeping it private. But yes, it is with her." I winked and Reese continued to stare at me.

"I'm happy for you. Sad for me, but happy for you. Good luck, Trent. If things change, you have my number."

"Bye, Casey."

I disconnected the call, tossed my phone back onto the arm of the couch, and grabbed a handful of popcorn knowing a gorgeous blonde sat next to me dumbfounded.

"Um... care to explain?"

"Are we not in a relationship?"

"I mean, I suppose so."

My left shoulder lifted to my ear. "Well, there you go. Now she knows. And she's keeping it off the record. Any other questions? Because I'd be more than happy to call every female in my contact list and tell them the same."

"No need." She could try and repress her glee as much as she wanted. I knew the woman next to me better than she thought. And what I also knew was, she owned my heart.

Reese's grandparents' home was beautiful. A bit bigger than mine, and where some of my wood trim had been painted, theirs was highlighted, making it look more opulent. Her grandfather stood in the den, watching a college game replay with a notebook in his hand. Mr. Reese looked more like a coach on a sideline on game day than an owner in his home.

"Hi, Grandad," Reese said, walking into the room.

"Sweetheart." He muted the TV and pulled her into an embrace, never letting go of his notebook. "So glad you could make it. Your grandmother had to run to the market but should be back any minute." His eyes met mine. "Trent, it's good to see you. How's your leg?"

"Hi, sir. Getting stronger every day."

I no longer had an immobilizing brace or my crutches. Instead, I had a smaller support around my knee and walking on it felt exhilarating. Scary the things we took for granted. We shook hands and Reese looked around him at the screen.

"Watching the Portland game again?"

He nodded. "Yes, you know me. What do you know about Cullen?"

This was the part where my girl accelerated. I just needed to keep my excitement to a minimum, considering where we were.

Reese began rattling off stats. Then added,

"He's good but takes too long in the pocket. Also, uses a four-step drop; his snap to release average is four point one seconds." I knew mine, and as though she heard my thoughts, she turned to me. "Two point one and a three step drop. Unless there's a blitz, then that changes things."

Damn.

Her grandfather chuckled. Reese went on to comment about the other quarterback on the opposing team. His stats were much better than Cullen's. "Thanks sweetheart." He clicked off the TV. "Enough shop talk. Let's get you both something to drink."

Just then the door swung open and a woman with light hair that rested on her shoulders walked in. I immediately recognized her as Reese's grandmother. They had the same almond-shaped blue eyes. Right behind her, her sister and brother-in-law walked in with Bubba resting in Kenzie's arms. That was until he saw me and started squirming.

Reese squatted with her arms open ready to scoop up the furball, but to her surprise, he ran straight to me. Lifting him, and doing my best not to tweak my knee, I let his small pink tongue bathe my jaw. "Hey, Bubba. How are ya, boy?" I scratched him behind his ears.

"Traitor." Reese's over-emphasized glower made everyone laugh.

After formal introductions were done, Kenzie

took Bubba from me and set him on the floor. She couldn't have been more different than her sister with dark hair and brown eyes, but their bond had been evident in the way they seemed to communicate without words. At one point, I almost felt naked, as I took a long pull from my beer.

Dave walked up to me. "Scary aren't they? I swear when Kenz and I first got together, it was as if they had their own language."

Still staring at Reese, I nodded. "They are pretty though."

"Yeah, they're gorgeous." Then he turned toward me wearing a serious expression. "Don't hurt her."

"I wouldn't dream of it."

The rest of the evening had been filled with stories from when the girls were little to idle meaningless conversation. It had been the most refreshing few hours I'd had in a very long time. Aside from her grandfather asking me how my knee was, no one else had mentioned it. *Thank God.*

We said our goodbyes and headed out to the car. Once inside, and safely buckled into the passenger seat, I turned to Reese. "Thank you for tonight. I had a great time."

"I'm glad, I did too."

Since my house was less than a quarter of a mile away, it took mere minutes to pull into my driveway. Reese parked the car, turned it off, and came around to my side. I knew she wanted to help me, but I needed her to know that I was fine.

Holding her face between the palms of my hands, I leaned down and kissed her. Reese's body practically molded to the side of the car as her back arched.

"I want you so much," I breathed out between kisses.

"I want you too."

Forcing myself to pull away, I looked into her eyes. "Stay the night with me?"

Reese wordlessly nodded and a shot of adrenaline rushed through me. So much so, I wanted to hoist her over my shoulder and carry her in caveman style. Instead, I laced my fingers with hers, and walked her inside, knowing that once we stepped through the door, she would be mine.

Finally.

19

Reese

HIS KISSES HAD BEEN ENOUGH to set me off like... as much as I hated to say it... a rocket. The thing about Trent, beyond the obvious, was his dedication to the task at hand. Right now that task was us. And speaking of hands, his were strong, confident, and touched me with the reverence I assumed he touched a football with.

Standing in his room, all thoughts of his injury were put aside. The animosity I had toward him, gone. All that remained was how much this man meant to me. Never in my life had I felt so close to someone in such a short amount of time—especially someone I'd put on a no-way-in-hell list. When Kenzie met Dave, she told me he was *the one* after their second date. Naturally, I didn't believe her. Those feelings were something out of the movies we had been watching—not reality.

Except, I started to get it now. To understand how Kenzie felt with Dave because all I wanted to do was crawl inside Trent's heart and pitch a tent. And from the way it beat against mine and from what he had been saying over the past weeks, my guess was he felt the same.

"What are you thinking about?" His breath against the soft spot beneath my ear had me writhing with need.

"Us," I simply answered, running my hands up his strong arms. My head limply fell to the left, giving him more real estate to work with, which he completely took advantage of.

"My favorite subject." His hands worked the hem of my sweater until it was up and over my head. He took a moment from ravishing my neck to stare at my red bra. It wasn't lacey or anything overly sexy. I chose it because it matched my sweater, and I was weird about coordinating undergarments with my clothes. And the cotton covered my size B boobs. In a flash, and with one flick of his fingers on my back, the band on my bra loosened.

"Impressive." I didn't want to think how often he'd practiced that move. Because I had a feeling that just like on the gridiron, Trent Archer didn't fumble in the bedroom either.

Hating to lose the feel of his body near mine,

but needing to even the playing field, I took a step back, curled my fingers at the edge of his T-shirt, and slowly raised it, giving my knuckles the pleasure of traveling up the muscular planes of his body. Starting at the apropos Adonis belt that framed his hips, my hands took their time wandering north until Trent took over and tossed his shirt aside.

"Do you realize how gorgeous you are?" His thumb grazed over my cheek and down to my lower lip. "I'm the luckiest man on earth."

"Believe me, you're the gorgeous one."

After another searing kiss, I carefully helped him out of his pants. "Are you sure you're up for this?" His eyes looked down at his boxers. When his gaze met mine, he cocked a brow. "You know what I mean. Your knee."

"I'm fine." Trent stripped me and then discarded his last piece of clothing before sitting on the edge of the bed. He pointed to the nightstand. Knowing what he wanted, I opened the drawer, pulled out a foil packet and handed it to him. Once ready, he pulled me on top of him so my legs straddled his waist. "See, no pressure on my knee whatsoever."

"Are you handing the ball off to me, Mr. QB?"

"Can you handle it?"

"Are you suggesting I may fumble?"

"Not a shot."

"Good." I smirked and pulled him closer right before taking us to the proverbial end zone.

My body ached in the most delicious of ways as I reached my hands toward the tufted headboard. Glancing to my right, ready to see the man who was responsible for my post-coital bliss, my expectation fell short when he wasn't there. Oddly, I could still feel him as though he were.

Last night surpassed anything I'd ever imagined sex could be. Don't get me wrong, I'm not a virgin, but I might as well have been since Trent took my body to places it had never dared to dream it could go. So many times Alexa would tell me about how she saw stars after the big O. How her body felt as though she were levitating. I laughed at how often I'd roll my eyes or wonder if she should write a fiction book, considering her embellishments seemed a bit unrealistic.

Except now… thanks to Trent, I knew they weren't. It made me wonder if the next time would be even better. Wanting to put that theory to the test, I tossed the covers aside, sat up, and glanced around the room. The bathroom door was open, but no sound of running water or anything to indicate Trent was there. Odd, after the night we had together. Feeling a bit groggy and in need of coffee, I picked up my phone, noticing a missed call from Alexa and a text from Trent stating he had to go to the Rockets' facility for a meeting. Since he still couldn't drive, Jackson was picking him up.

Finally, pulling myself out of bed, I snagged a hair tie out of my purse, hustled into the bathroom, cleaned up as best as I could, tossed my hair up in a haphazard ponytail, and rinsed my mouth with his minty mouthwash on the vanity. Stepping back out into his room, I glanced at the messy bed before noticing my clothes placed neatly on the chair in the corner of Trent's room.

I quickly got dressed, made his bed, grabbed my phone, and headed down the stairs. The smell of coffee acted as a magnetic force, yanking me into the kitchen. When I turned the corner, my hand flew to my chest.

"Good morning, you must be Reese. I'm Lily," the older woman putting on her coat said before adding, "I'm sorry I startled you. I was just about to head out. Trent said he left you a note that he went to the facility?"

"Hi, Lily. It's a pleasure to meet you. And yes, he sent me a text."

"May I get you something before I go? Coffee, maybe?"

"Thanks anyway, but I should get going." Out of the corner of my eye, I spotted Trent's phone on the island.

She must have followed my line of vision

because Lily nodded as she slipped the last button through the hole on her coat. "He forgot it and his keys. I'd drop them off, but I'm not heading in that direction."

I wasn't either, but that didn't stop me from picking them up. "I can do it."

"Great. I'm sure he'll appreciate it." I grabbed the rest of my things, we both walked out, and after Lily locked up, we headed to our cars before saying goodbye.

Pulling out onto the road, I drove past my grandparents' home and took the main thoroughfare until I got to the highway.

Thankfully, traffic wasn't horrible, and I didn't have too far to travel. Before I knew it, I was parked in front of the Rockets' training facility and home office. The arched arena building connected to a taller structure where the business offices were housed by way of a pedestrian bridge. It wasn't much different than the Thunder's except our training facility had an underground tunnel that connected the two structures. Either way, theirs boasted a more modern vibe.

Glancing around, I noticed there weren't a lot of cars in the lot. Maybe the players parked in a different area. However, the season was over, so maybe they were meeting with Trent's trainer? Whatever the case was, I had to give him his phone and keys.

Before I got out of my car, I lowered my visor,

horrified by the leftover eyeliner I still had under my eyes. I grabbed a tissue and a bottle of leftover water that I kept in my car, and used both to remove the dark shadow. I swiped my lips with pink gloss, tossed a baseball cap on my head, one with the Thunder's logo of course, and exited my car.

I couldn't help but laugh, knowing when Trent saw my hat he'd get a kick out of it. Maybe it was my way of breaking the ice after the night we spent together. Granted he probably didn't want to wake me up this morning, but better that then looking haggard when I saw him. Except... too late now.

After pulling open the door to the training facility I expected to hear the rumbles of voices or any type of sound, but the only ambient noise was provided by the overhead HVAC units. Not sure where to go, rather than head out, I walked around the practice field, and opened two double doors, half expecting to find a security guard but didn't.

I made my way down the navy and gray carpeted hallway, and thanks to the door cracked open a bit, I heard the sound of Trent's voice, and headed in that direction happy that I'd found him. The smile on my face died a quick death when I heard him say, "What do you mean, no offer?" My heart slammed against my ribcage, my fingers gripped my purse strap slung across my body. I knew I shouldn't stand there, but I was scared to move. Why would the Rockets not sign him? They just won the final championship game, and Trent was the league's best. The MVP for crying out loud... or in this case whispering in my head.

"Like Charlie told you, the scans don't show the tear healing as quickly as they hoped. That along with three doctors all recommending not to play for another nine months, some even saying never..." My hand flew over my mouth in shock. I couldn't be sure who had just delivered that news, but something told me it was Dane Conti their GM. I'd met him and his wife once at a charity event and had seen them a couple of times afterward. He was friends with my granddad. "We need a quarterback, Trent."

Another voice said, "If you push yourself too much too early, you could do permanent damage to your leg. Not to mention, despite this concussion being minor, it was still a concussion."

"I'm fine and you both are overreacting." Annoyance mixed with sadness in Trent's voice brought tears to my eyes. "Look, I'll sit out the first few months. Troy can easily step in."

"Trent, you're not hearing us, so, I'll say it a bit clearer..." Yes, that was definitely Dane. He had a bit of a New England accent and it had just come through. "As of today, Troy Davis is the Rockets starting quarterback. You've brought so much to this game, sport, and the team can't thank you enough for your dedication, but you are no longer on the Rockets' roster. I'm sorry, Trent." *Oh my God.*

Something crashed right before the door swung open. I had lost my window to do the right thing and walk away before getting caught eavesdropping. It hadn't been my intent, but when Trent's eyes landed on mine, the joy in my heart I had woken up with faltered.

"Hi. Um… you left your phone and keys on the counter." I reached into my bag, grabbed them, then stretched my hand out, holding his things, and all he did was stare at my hand. Suddenly, I felt like Baby in *Dirty Dancing* and may as well have said, "I carried a watermelon."

His agent, who I knew to be Sam Jasper, walked out. He glanced at me before turning to a pissed-off Trent. "We have options. My job is to make sure you land on your feet. I'll call you later. The details will be emailed to you. We can discuss it more then."

Other than a single nod, Sam never vocally acknowledged me. He definitely knew who I was. Except, I wasn't worried about him. My concern was for the man in front of me, who just twelve hours ago seemed to have everything going for him, and now looked broken.

I'd been in my granddad's office before when the GM had to break bad news to a player. It was awful. Consulting was one thing. Being in the room while someone's lifelong dream was coming true, even better. Telling someone they were essentially fired — that was something completely different, and nothing I wanted any part of.

Rather than spew words I knew would only sound pitiful, I wrapped my arms around him.

His hand smoothed the back of my ponytail until it landed on my spine. "You heard?"

Nodding into his chest, I sadly whispered, "Yes. I'm sorry, Trent."

I felt his lungs expand with a deep breath. He exhaled and released his hold on me and took my hand in his. We went through a different door and were met with a set of stairs. When he took a step, he winced. "Is it your knee?" I stupidly blurted.

"My knee is fine." My head reared back at his curtness that echoed in the dank stairwell. "Seriously, I know how I feel. Doctors can say what they want, but they're wrong."

"They're only doing what's best for you, Trent."

"Yeah. Well, Idaho has shown interest. As has Oklahoma. If either of those teams make me an offer, I'd be more than happy to be in the same division as the Rockets. Actually, I'd prefer it."

Those states were clear across the country. Despite knowing professional athletes went where the spots were, the thought of Trent so far away saddened me. More than that, the thought of Trent doing worse damage to his knee or his head gave me pause. Maybe being released was the best thing for him. Naturally, I kept that thought to myself.

When we made it to the bottom, Trent led me through another door, tossed his arm around my shoulder and kissed the top of my head. "I'm sorry, I snapped. You didn't deserve that. I'm also sorry for all of this. Believe me, I much rather have stayed in bed this morning with my girlfriend."

Girlfriend. I wished that too. "Next time."

"Damn, straight. Look, I need to clear out my locker and grab my things. Jackson is in the gym. He has no idea this happened, but I need to talk to him. Do you mind if I just walk you out?"

"It's fine, I should get home, I'm very… stale. Just point me in the right direction."

"Babe, you look perfect to me." His eyes glanced up and that smirk that used to annoy me, but now made my body spark to life, appeared. "Nice hat, by the way."

"Thank you, it's my favorite. Lily put a few meals for you in the fridge." *Next to the cold pack,* I wanted to add but didn't.

"Oh, before you go…" Trent's strong hands palmed my face as he drew me in and softly kissed me. Every part of my body came to life. This man enthralled me with his touch, enticed me with the mere graze of his hand, and his kisses undid me. I wanted to take him up on his previous comment about going back to bed, but I did need to leave.

Our connection broke and Trent gave me his signature wink that in some way felt as though it were just for me. That no other woman experienced it the way I had. It was also nice to see the Trent I started to fall for come back. "I'll call you later. And Reese, don't tell anyone about what happened here today."

"Never even crossed my mind."

He took his phone and keys from me, gave me one more axis-tilting kiss, and sent me on my way.

20

Trent

MY LIFE WENT FROM BEING absolutely amazing to *are you freaking kidding me?* Something told me when Dane called this morning, wanting to meet, I should have postponed and stayed in bed with Reese. Waking up with the ends of her soft blonde hair on part of my pillow felt like a dream. It made me wish it was an everyday occurrence.

Even when I went to the facility, the thought of the Rockets releasing me had never crossed my mind. Conversely, when he said he wanted to discuss things in person, it should have been a clue. Probably because I woke up on cloud nine, nothing remotely negative had been on my mind.

Last night with Reese had been more than I had hoped for. The way her body responded to mine as though she were made for me... as though we were made for each other. I could still hear her moans and smell her sweet perfume as we lay together. My hands flexed at the mere memory of how her soft skin felt like a soothing balm.

Then I left, and my world turned upside down.

Never had I thought that being summoned to a meeting would result in my unemployment. The idea of not playing football for the Rockets, a team that had been my family for the past five years, not only saddened me, but pissed me off. Hearing Dane say it wasn't only in the team's best interest but my own, almost had me coming unglued. If Sam hadn't been in the room, I may have done that.

Then when I left and saw Reese in the hallway, a wave of total uncertainty washed over me.

Reese.

I couldn't help but wonder what was going through her mind. The *old* Reese, the one pre-phenomenal sex Reese, would have been all over this. She and Alexa probably would have made cookies with my number crossed out by a big red X on them. Those probably would have been the next top seller after the crazy bird ones.

Now what did she think? Reese knew the game like the back of her hand. I was sure she'd witnessed many a player being fired or at least heard about it. Maybe that was one of the reasons why she didn't like working in the office, well, except for when it came to the draft. Thinking about the woman I knew now, that made total sense. She'd rather make someone's day than destroy it. Except for our first encounter. No, take that back. In retrospect, she did make someone's day — mine.

Pushing through the locker room door, I strolled over to the one with my last name above it, stuffed my belongings into a duffle bag, and picked up the football I kept since my first day in DC. Glancing at the oval pigskin with the number two etched on it, I tossed it across the room until it landed in the center of a garbage can.

"Whoa. What's going on here?" Jackson strolled in, glanced at the can, and looked at me. "Just ran into Reese. I happened to be in the parking lot grabbing something from my car."

"What did she say? That her boyfriend got cut from the Rockets because they think he's done?"

His hands went up, then his right one reached into the garbage and picked up my ball.

"First, back up." He ran his fingers through his hair and pitched his free hand on his waist. "I'll get back to the boyfriend comment, but did you say you got cut? All she said was you were done with your meeting. Didn't say why or what it was about."

I puffed out my cheeks and exhaled right before picking up my duffle. "Sorry, man. I am. But all of this caught me off guard. Do you mind if we get out of here? I'll explain everything when we get to my place."

He nodded, grabbed his own bag, and we headed out. When I glanced back, I realized this was the last time I'd be in this room. Although it should have felt like a kick to the nuts, something about it told me I'd be back. Maybe not as a Rocket, but in one way or another, this team hadn't seen the last of me.

I got up, walked to the fridge, and pulled out a beer. "Want one?"

"It's not even noon yet."

After the cap had been popped, I took a long pull. Cool liquid stung my throat as I swallowed a few gulps. Setting the bottle down, I shook my head. "Sorry, man. I'm just shocked."

"You're the only one who's thrown to me since college." He shook his head. "On second thought, screw it. I got no place to be, and it's five o'clock somewhere, right?"

I grabbed another beer, popped the cap, and handed it to him. Before he took a sip, we tapped the necks together. We didn't have anything to toast to, so instead, I answered his question. "Damn, straight."

Needing to know if it had hit the media yet, we went into the family room, sat in our usual places, and clicked on the television.

Highlights from last night's basketball game

were on, then they moved to college hoops before hockey fodder. "Maybe they don't know."

Shrugging, I was about to change the channel when the ticker on the bottom of the screen flashed and white letters highlighted in red scrawled across it stating: FREE AGENT QUARTERBACK AND CHAMPIONSHIP MVP, TRENT ARCHER, IS NO LONGER WITH THE DC ROCKETS.

The host turned his chair to face a different camera, his left hand touched his ear, and then he reported the news. "I just got word that the DC Rockets will not be re-signing their star and once franchised player, and quite frankly one of the best players in the league, Trent Archer."

"Unreal," Jackson muttered.

"We'll have more information on our evening broadcast but for now all we know is Archer is out, and Troy Davis will be in as the Rockets new QB. Stay with us, we'll be back after this short break."

A lump formed in my throat. *Out.* I couldn't believe it.

When I glanced at Jackson, he looked as though he had been kicked in the gut. "Troy's good, you'll be fine," I said to him.

He nodded and took a swig of his beer. "Yeah, I know. Except, you're my guy. As soon as you land somewhere, I'm asking to be traded."

"They're not going to trade you. You're one of the best ends in the league."

"Fine, but next year when my contract is up, it'll be the Archer and Cartwright show. We're like peanut butter and jelly. They're okay alone, but together, they're the best."

I laughed. "Thanks, man. And yeah, wherever I land, I'll be sure to get you there."

We raised our bottles, took a sip, and for the first time since I heard the news, I started to feel a bit better. "What about the Thunder? Donnelly should be announcing his retirement soon. At least you'd be in the area."

"Yeah, maybe. I wouldn't want to make Reese uncomfortable. But you're right. I'll mention it to Sam."

The thought of playing for the Thunder gave me a bit of hope. Finally for the first time since that morning, I started to feel a little more positive. Maybe it will all work out after all.

"Hey, so change of topic?" he asked with a small smile on his face. "Girlfriend? You two are official?"

Of all the guys I knew, Jackson was the one who would most likely settle down. Unless they were already married, most players were just that—on and off the field. Despite Jackson having a bevy of beauties at his beck and call, he rarely dialed a number. I'm sure he wasn't celibate by any means, but if I were going to discuss a relationship with any of the guys, he'd be the only one I knew for certain wouldn't talk me out of it.

Commitment meant a lot to him. It was one of the reasons we meshed so well. Our friendship was the longest relationship I've had outside of my family. He was right, for the past five years he had been my go-to guy on and off the field. When I moved, that would end too. Not our friendship, but that comradery we shared. Who knew if I'd ever find that with another player?

"I like her a lot. She's sexy as hell, gorgeous, loves football, feisty…" *Great in bed.* I left that out because that was information not to be shared. "And smart."

"Good for you. I'll give it to her, that woman had me at *middle finger hoisted in the air.*" I chuckled. "All the cookies aren't bad either."

"Well, that's more Alexa and her mom."

"Another stunning chick."

"Erica? Yeah, she's pretty…" I trailed off because I'd seen the way he flirted with Alexa.

"Glad you haven't lost your sense of humor."

I tilted my head with a tight smile before taking another sip of my beer. Glancing around my house, I wondered if I'd still be living here in a couple months.

"So, what now? I know this is all fresh and maybe you should take a day or two, but we both know that won't happen."

He was right. Draft day wasn't far away. Team owners and GMs already had their favorites. If I wanted to land a starting job, I needed to do it sooner than later. "I'll call Sam and have him reach out to a couple interested teams. Meanwhile, I'll schedule a meeting with Charles Reese."

"Will you tell Bird? I mean your girlfriend?"

Will I? "No. This is business. If her grandfather wants to discuss it with her, that's his decision. Mr. Reese brought me to this town and hopefully he'll want to keep me here."

Jackson nodded. He grabbed the remote and turned off the television. "Pool?"

I stood. "Yeah, now that I know my girlfriend is a hustler, best to practice." He laughed, and I knew he didn't want me in front of the television where my career would most certainly be discussed. Jackson racked the balls, chalked his cue, and leaned over the table. "Hey, thanks for this."

Jackson didn't need to say anything and for the next few hours the only thing I worried about was not hitting the eight ball.

21
Reese

"**T**HANK YOU, MRS. LANCASTER," I said, handing the kind woman her change, letting the coins rattle in the drawer as I closed it.

"We'll be seeing you at the Pink and Black Gala this year, won't we, dear?"

That event had been one I'd attended since I was a teenager. My granddad had always instilled giving beyond receiving. The Pink and Black had been one of my favorites, in part to the pretty gray-haired woman in front of me. It benefited the Kids Around the Corner, a charity that gave tuition to kids who couldn't afford to go to sport camps. Mrs. Lancaster's grandfather started it. When he was younger, he'd been one of those kids. After he passed away, his family made sure to continue his work.

The first time I went to the gala was unforgettable. The room looked magical all decorated in, of course, pink and black. Gorgeous pastel floral arrangements and flickering gold candles adorned the tables. It looked like something out of a fairy tale. Even the guests in their gowns and tuxedos played a role in make-believe becoming reality.

Most of the people were adults, however Mrs. Lancaster pulled me aside to introduce me to her neighbor. That was the day I met Alexa. A smile split my face as I recalled a dark-haired girl around my age talking to a boy who appeared to be high school age. Always a flirt that one.

"Yes, of course. I may even have a date this time." I winked.

"Yep, she's ditching me for a hot man," Alexa teased, plopping a hand on her cocked hip. "Can you believe that?"

Mrs. Lancaster laughed. "Oh, you girls are so silly. I can always count on you to brighten my day. I'll see you both later."

Alexa's expression morphed from gleeful to the opposite. "Have you talked to him yet? I don't follow the sport but it's all I'm hearing about. Even satellite radio DJs are announcing it."

"No, I haven't talked to him since yesterday. He sent me a text that he was hanging out with Jackson. Plus, I'm not exactly sure what to say. I don't want to make him feel worse by asking dumb questions, like, *how are you?* when I know he's anything but good. It's like asking me if I'm cold when it's less than sixty degrees outside."

She nodded. "I feel really bad for him."

"I do too. We had such a great night and then morning came, I woke up alone, and the you-know-what hit the fan."

Her hand went into the air. "Uh… hold on one second, Missy. Are you telling me that you and that gorgeous man sealed the deal, and I'm just finding out now?"

My cheeks warmed with her question. "You know I don't kiss and tell."

"Reese Parker, I'm insulted." Her eyes darted around the empty bakery. "It was great though, right?"

A ringing sound came from my pocket just as my mouth opened to tell her that he was the best I'd ever had. Not that I'd had a lot, but if he were the last man I made love to, I wouldn't be disappointed. Plucking out my cell, I saw my granddad's picture I kept as his contact.

"Hi, Granddad."

"Hi, sweetheart. I hope I'm not interrupting you."

"No, you're not interrupting." I glanced at Alexa who undoubtedly disagreed with me.

"Can you come down to the office? We're going over a few stats and profiles for the draft. We could use your mind."

"I see. In other words, your staff is driving you crazy."

"Did I say that?" He chuckled.

"Okay, I can come there. Give me about an hour?"

"Sounds good. Thanks, honey."

"My pleasure."

When I slid the phone into the back pocket of my jeans, Alexa crossed her arms in front of her chest. "If that was anyone but your grandfather, you wouldn't be going anywhere."

I giggled and took off my apron. As I hung it on the hook before walking into the break room to get my things, I turned and threw my friend a tantalizing tidbit. "The best I've ever had."

Right before the door closed I heard her exclaim, "I knew it!"

Grandpa's office buzzed with activity. People wearing headphones talking animatedly also indicated the intensity of free agents, trades before the draft, predictions of what would be done during the draft, and any other instances that may cause a stir. Unless you worked for the organization, people thought the season started in August and ended after the final game. When in fact, like other businesses, it operated year-round.

I said hello to a few people who simply nodded. When I saw my granddad's assistant, relief flashed across her face. "Hi, Isabelle."

She let out a breath. "Hi, sweetie. Your grandfather is expecting you. Go right in. I was just about to head out for lunch. He had lunch brought in for you both."

"Thanks." I knocked once before entering. My granddad sat at a small round table. Piles of paper were stacked and lined up. God forbid he did this all on his computer. No, that would be Isabelle's job, once he decided what to do. He said it was easier to shift things around manually. I suppose he was right. Plus, who was I to buck a system that had been working for decades?

"There she is." He stood and pulled me into his arms. The familiar scent of his cologne reminded me of home and warmed me better than a cozy fire. "Thanks for coming in."

"My pleasure." I shrugged off my coat, hung it over the back of the chair, and sat down. "So, who are we looking at today?"

"First…" He turned and let out a breath. "I heard about Trent."

I nodded sullenly. "Yeah, that was a shock."

"I'd say. Never saw that coming."

"No one did."

When I glanced at the table, I saw we were starting with special team players. Unlike my granddad, I pulled my tablet out of my bag, and brought up who I liked. Idaho had a tremendous kicker who hadn't missed a field goal under fifty-three yards last season. Then there was a returner from Arkansas who only played his last two years in college because he got a scholarship in track before he made the switch to football.

For the next two hours, we watched some films, read more stats, debated a few players, and came up with a game plan for our special teams, defense, and our offensive line. Now came the hard part. A quarterback. The leader of the team needed to be someone special. Someone respected by everyone and not someone who thought more of themselves than the team. That was why I wanted to skip over the cocky quarterback that most teams were drooling over.

"Donnelly will be announcing his retirement at the end of the week."

"He gave good years to the team."

"Yes, we'll be celebrating that on Friday night. Don't forget the Pink and Black Gala is coming up."

"I'll be there. Hopefully, with Trent."

Granddad rubbed his chin, sat back in his chair, and tossed the pencil he held in his hand onto the table. "Tell me about Trent." I felt my face flame, which for some reason he thought was funny. "I meant about how he's feeling."

"I'm not sure what you're asking me."

"We need a quarterback. Trent's available. I know the doctors are saying six to nine months, but we can figure it out. If it's six months, it brings us to the beginning of the pre-season. We have Carter who can lead us until then. And before you say it, yes, I know Carter isn't the best. But if we have the best waiting, we'll make do for now. In your honest opinion, tell me what you think."

I stood and began to pace. A silent debate went on in my head, but in all honesty, no debating had been necessary. There was only one answer I could give my granddad. The only one that made sense.

Straightening my spine, I rolled my shoulders back, and said with the utmost confidence. "I would draft or try and trade for either Mitchell Grayson from Phoenix or Drake Reynolds from Wisconsin to be our quarterback, but I wouldn't bring Trent on as a starter. I'm not sure I'd bring him on at all."

Movement in the doorway caught my attention. When I turned, I expected to see Isabelle. Instead, Trent stood there looking shocked and disappointed... again. The same look I'd seen yesterday reappeared. Except this time those feelings were because of me.

"Trent?"

I watched his Adam's apple drop down his throat in a hefty swallow. When he didn't say anything, my granddad stood. That must have pulled him out of wherever his thought had taken him because he shook his head. "Hi, Mr. Reese. I wanted to come and talk to you about a future with your team, but I see that your consultant has already discussed it with you."

"Son, come in and have a seat."

Trent shook his head again. "No, thank you though. I wish you a great season. Good luck in the draft."

When he turned and walked away, tears immediately filled my eyes. With blurred vision, I practically had to run to catch up to him.

"Trent, wait. Let me explain."

A few employees looked on with curiosity. Not wanting an audience, I pulled him into an empty office and closed the door.

"You want to explain? You want to tell me why you, my girlfriend, told her grandfather not to bring me on as the team's quarterback when you both know I'm the best in the league? Is this payback for not signing on with you five years ago?"

"What? No! That's not —"

"I can't believe this." He moved and let out a slight grimace.

"It's that. Your health. That's what it is. I'm not willing to risk your health for our wins. If you want to go sign on with another team, by all means go do it. But I heard that your knee isn't healing as well as it should be. I also heard that another concussion wouldn't be good. Not that I didn't already know that."

"So you made it personal? You took the knowledge you knew as my girlfriend and used it against me."

"No, that's not it." I reached for him but he pulled his arm away from my touch. "I did it because I care about you" — *and I think I'm falling in love with you* — "and don't want to see you risk further injury."

He inhaled in a huff. "This is caring to you?" My chin quivered and all I could do was stare. "If you *cared,* you would know I need this in my life. I'm a quarterback. It's what I know and what I live for."

I wanted to say he was so much more than a quarterback, but I knew enough about the man not to go there. A deep-rooted part of me also wanted to say, let *us* be who you live for, but I didn't, instead tears clogged my throat because when it came down to it, it was his life that concerned me. Then anger simmered and my heart slammed against my ribs in a rhythmic dance. "Did you know that over sixty-five percent of fatalities among football players are due to brain injuries? Do you know how terrifying that is to me? To everyone who loves you? So you can think what you want, but it's because of how *much* I care that I can't be the one responsible. I'm sorry."

Trent rolled his lips between his teeth. I noticed his deep scruff and the dark circles under his eyes. He probably hadn't slept since we were together.

His beautiful green eyes lacked the sparkle they usually held, then they locked onto mine, and rather than seeing adoration or even like, I saw the opposite. "You made this personal, Reese. This isn't about statistics that you love to spout. I'm fine. It was a mild concussion, that's it. And as far as my knee, you wouldn't have known what was said if you weren't my girlfriend at the time."

At the time?

I could literally feel a deep burning inside of my chest, but I did my best to hold it together. The look in his eyes matched the way he scrubbed his jaw before massaging the back of his neck. Did he realize what he'd said? He just told me we were no longer together. All I could do was stare.

"I'll catch on with another team." When he paused I half thought—no prayed—he'd apologize for his gruffness. Maybe even take back the *at the time* comment. Instead all he said was, "See ya 'round."

He turned on his heel and strode out of the office, leaving me alone with my shattered heart. Despite the pain I felt, and the fact that I truly did care about him, I'd rather see him walk away than hurt himself. Except, as he disappeared down the hallway, he took a piece of my heart with him... one I knew I'd never get back.

22

Trent

THE NERVE. LEAVE IT TO Reese to start rattling off stats. I knew the dangers of the sport, and I took all necessary precautions. I had no headaches, no nausea, or any other concussion symptoms. Yeah, my knee didn't feel fantastic, but I'd been icing and elevating it like the doc instructed. Plus, I could walk on it with barely a limp. "Six to nine months," I scoffed to no one, since it was just me at my place.

Jackson offered to come over, but I wasn't in the mood for company. The last time I was on edge my mother told me she had breast cancer. Not being able to control what was happening annoyed the hell out of me. Life. Just when you think you're on top of the world, you get punched in the gut.

My phone rang for the tenth time in the past thirty minutes. Not wanting to talk to anyone, I'd been ignoring it. But when I saw Sam's name, I tapped the green button and raised it to my ear.

"Give me good news."

"Hello to you too," he blandly said. When I didn't offer a different greeting, he went on to say, "Phoenix wants to see you in three weeks. They know about your knee and will work around the situation. But they still want to have a conversation and of course have their trainer look at you. Preliminary numbers as far as salary is good. Not as good as DC, but it keeps you in the league. As always, I'll put in performance incentives. Also, *Sports News Daily* wants an interview as does *Fifty Yard Line Reports.* Both will give you great airtime to tell your side of things. For now, that's all I have. Hopefully, that will improve your day."

I exhaled and felt a little of the weight sitting on my chest lift. "Thanks, Sam. Sorry, for acting like a jackass. Along with everything else, I had a run-in with Reese and it didn't end well."

"I spoke to Charles. He said there wouldn't be an offer from the Thunder. Sorry about Reese."

"Yeah. Me too. Anything else?"

"I'll let you know about any and all interest. Oh, and before I forget, the Pink and Black Gala benefitting the Kids Around the Corner is coming up." The last thing I wanted to do was go to an event. As though reading my mind, he went on to say, "I know that's probably the last place you want to be, but it will be good press if people see you out and about. It will negate some of the speculation that you're not even walking around yet."

"Who said that?" I barked. "You know what, never mind. I'll be there."

"One more thing?"

"Go on."

"Reese will most likely be there too since the Thunder are a sponsor. As will the executives from the Rockets."

"Right. I'll behave."

"That's what I wanted to hear."

"Wanna be my date?"

He chuckled. "You mean babysitter? I'll pass. Bye Trent. Everything will be fine."

"See ya."

Fine. Would it be? I wasn't sure. Twenty-four hours ago I had a job and a girlfriend. Now, I had neither. And that girlfriend was part of the reason for losing both. Well, maybe not the latter, *that* was on me. The hurt in her eyes felt like a dagger to my heart, but it had already been wounded with the words I heard her tell her grandfather.

Needing a shower, I made my way up the stairs with little to no pain, and begrudgingly walked into my bedroom. Reese's perfume still hung in the air. An image of her lying in my bed would forever be tattooed on my brain. Picturing her naked and in my arms while we made love forced me to sit heavily in that same spot. I dropped my head in my hands, wishing things could have turned out differently.

Who would have thought that woman in the end zone who gave me the finger would be the woman I'd fallen in love with? That same woman who with a few words ended my chances to stay in DC. She said she cared. If she did, wouldn't she realize how I couldn't easily walk away? And that I'd do everything in my power to stay in the league? Which meant, I'd most likely move away from her. Clearly that probability hadn't crossed her mind. Conversely it has been in the forefront of mine.

I stripped out of my clothes and cranked on my shower. When the water was a tolerable temp, I stepped inside and let it beat down on my skin. I adjusted the knob to turn on the rain shower heads attached to the ceiling, sat on the teak bench, laid my head back on the tile, and hoped when I stepped out things would be better.

Except, I knew this wasn't Narnia. Our lives weren't like those cheesy movies Reese and I watched together. Life was tough, and as much as I wanted to believe we could have had it all, we didn't live in a fairy tale. When we first started to see one another, I had a feeling she would change my life.

Boy did she ever.

Back then, I hoped that one day I'd call her mine. Who knew things would get so messed up? I turned the water off, stepped out of the shower, looked in the mirror, and wished things were back to normal. I wished she wasn't right about the All-Pro game. I wished I could have seen Beckett coming. I wished that things were back to the way they were. But too much had happened. I needed to be patient and wait to see what the future held. If nothing else, I'd move to California and be closer to my family.

My phone pulled me from my thoughts. I padded across the floor to my nightstand. Seeing my mom's face made me smile for the first time today.

"Hey, were your ears ringing?" I asked, shrugging on a T-shirt.

"Ahh, they were. Who were you talking to about me?"

"No one. Well, just myself. I was thinking I might move back there." I knew she heard the news because my dad had sent me a text to call when I was ready to talk. Apparently, Mom didn't get that memo.

"Trent Archer, I love you, but what about Reese?"

"We broke up. Long story, and I don't want to get into it." Despite my words, I did go ahead and rattle off the Cliffs Notes version.

"I agree with her. I know you're young and strong, but sweetheart, your health comes first. Except, I also know you and football. Just be smart. Don't let your pride ruin a good thing. There's nothing wrong with stepping away while you're on top. You don't have anything to prove to anyone."

Yes, she was half right. I didn't need to prove anything. Except, I wasn't ready to retire at twenty-eight. "Thanks, Mom. I appreciate that."

She laughed. "Just let me know what team to root for next."

"You've got it."

I sat on the bed, dried off my legs, and slipped on my elastic brace before putting on a pair of track pants. My first thought was to call Jackson to see if he wanted to go to the gala with me, but instead, I went downstairs and watched the sports channel to see what the latest was.

As soon as the commercial ended and the host finished talking about the draft, the meme of Reese and me popped up. I hadn't seen it in a while. Clicking the pause button, I stared at the screen. Everything about Reese was beautiful, even her upright finger. The glint in her eyes, the confident stance, and the way she didn't hold back letting me know exactly how she felt should have been a precursor to our relationship. What did she call the couple in that movie we watched? Enemies to lovers? I didn't understand it then, but I got it now. A couple of months ago, I was enemy number one to Reese. Funny how quickly those tables turned. The problem was, deep down, I'd much rather have her as my lover than my enemy.

Rather than continuing to torture myself, I unpaused the television, rested my head on the arm of the sofa, and stretched out, putting my right foot on a pillow. The announcers became white noise as I closed my eyes and fell asleep, hoping when I woke up things would make more sense. Except somehow, I knew that was a long shot.

23

Reese

IT HAD BEEN NINE DAYS since I last saw Trent in person. Naturally, his face had been all over the national and local sports broadcasts. There was still a deep ache in my heart, stemming from what might come of all that had transpired. Anytime I heard his name or saw his handsome face on the screen or online, sadness washed over me. Of course, the media caught on that we were no longer a couple. I hadn't been sure if it was out of pure speculation or if they got their intel from the source — meaning Trent.

No way on God's green earth could I visualize Trent going to the press about our personal life — I know I wouldn't. Nor would any of my friends or family. Yet, as usual, the news didn't go untold. Predictably, reporters like Veronica and Casey feasted on the gossip as a shark would on bait.

Still, regardless of everything, I wouldn't change what I said to Granddad. Nor would I change my mind when it came to the stubborn man who I had fallen in love with.

Part of me wished I could go back to that moment in the small office at Thunder's headquarters and tell him I was falling in love with him. On the other hand, how much more would it have hurt when he cast me aside? A lot more. Excruciatingly more. It had been agonizing having him walk away from me. Putting my heart on the line only to be squashed? Pass.

"What do you think of this one?" Alexa twirled in a long black gown that hugged her curves. When God doled out stunning figures to go with beautiful faces, he didn't pass her by. He also gifted her a compassionate heart, which in my opinion had to do with Him knowing she'd have me to deal with.

"I love it."

Since I had to make an appearance at the gala, Alexa agreed to be my plus-one. Truthfully, I didn't want to go. It was bad enough getting gloomy looks from the customers who came into the bakery. Being in a room full of people who most likely either felt sorry for me or thought I was an idiot would be ten times worse. *Sigh.* But thanks to my best friend, who said wallowing at home wouldn't do me any good, we were out shopping at a boutique.

"Let's find you one now."

"I might just wear something I have."

Her slender shoulders sagged. "No way. You need something fresh." She craned her head to look at her back in the three-way mirror before bringing her eyes back to me. "Is he going?"

I shrugged. "Not sure. My guess would be yes. It's a charity most athletes support."

"Then get your ass up before I start picking out dresses for you. Your grandfather gave you his credit card and said to have fun. This"—she waggled her pink-polished finger at me—"is not having fun. *This* is sulking. There's no sulking in shopping!"

"You're so—"

"Fabulous? Yes, I know."

Shimmying across the floor, she walked up to the rack of dresses the store's stylist picked out for us to try on. Some were sexier than others. Knowing that Alexa would pick a sexy-as-sin one, I spotted the opposite. A pretty true-pink cocktail dress that looked like something out of the 50s or 60s. It wasn't floor-length, but I instantly loved it. The material was soft, layers of tulle made the skirt flare like a bell. Small black flowers made of the same material, dotted the boat style neckline. I was instantly transported into a fairy tale. And since reality stunk at that moment, I might as well delve into fiction.

Taking it off the rack, I held it in front of me. Alexa took a step back, the material of her dress falling away at her leg thanks to the long slit on the front of it.

"Wow. That dress deserves amazing shoes."

The salesperson appeared out of nowhere probably seeing dollar signs flash. "What size are you?"

"Eight."

She nodded, took the dress from my hand, and told me it would be in room two. "Well, here goes nothing."

Alexa squealed but not before shouting to our saleswoman that she wore a seven and a half. When I glanced at her she smiled. "One can never have enough shoes."

Laughing for the first time in a while, I headed to room two and tried on the most perfect dress. The way the bodice hugged my torso felt heavenly. When I opened the door, the eager woman offered me two styles of shoes to try on. Opting for the black strappy heels, I sat down, slid them on, and stood. Everything about the ensemble made me feel special.

My best friend gasped. "Gorgeous." She circled me in her own stunning black heels. "Hair up, natural makeup, light contouring..." Alexa tapped her index finger on her chin and continued, "Dark eyeliner, pink glossy lips, and of course matching toes and nails. Mani/pedis are a must."

I nodded because she was right. My giddy friend and I changed back into our regular clothes while the saleswoman, who most likely made her weekly quota on our purchases, bagged everything for us. Once we had our new outfits, the two of us headed back to my place to indulge in my favorite Thai takeout and, of course, ice cream.

For the past couple of hours, and just like she'd been doing since my breakup with Trent, Alexa went out of her way to take my mind off of things... mainly him. Except, it wasn't an easy feat. How could it be when his name and face seemed to be everywhere? Fans of the Rockets had a petition going to get him back. Some protested with signs outside the stadium. And through it all, Trent had yet to make a statement.

At least a few times a day, I'd grab my phone, scroll to his contact info, open a text, and stare. Some days I would go as far as typing out a message only to delete it, one letter at a time. One time I almost accidentally sent it, which would have been horrible since it said that I loved him.

I wondered if I'd ever be able to tell him or if the one time I'd fallen in love would go without speaking the words I'd waited twenty-three years to say to a man. Except, anytime I thought about doing just that, he'd reciprocate in-kind.

"Sweetie, your ice cream is turning into soup."

"Sorry, my mind wandered."

"Let's watch a movie. Rom-com or horror?"

"Horror."

Alexa laughed and turned on the television. The channel had last been on a local one because I needed to know the weather, but rather than seeing a graphic of sun and clouds, a video of Trent at a local coffee shop seemed to be newsworthy. Leaning in a bit closer, my heart stuttered, watching him laugh. It was as though my heart grew little wings and a weight had been lifted. He was happy. Smiling. A whoosh of optimism filled my soul. Then when he stepped aside, I noticed a brunette next to him. The wings that had just sprouted stilled.

"Is that…?" Alexa asked, pulling the spoon out of her mouth.

"Yes, Casey McGrath."

"Ugh."

"Yeah, and I recently found out she's also his ex-fling."

"She's wretched looking." I scrunched up my nose. "Fine whatever, she's pretty, I guess if you're into that sort of look."

"Gorgeous, tall, a body that doesn't quit, and smart? Yeah, who could possibly be into that?"

As quickly as she turned the television on, she turned it off. "I'm sure it wasn't anything. Come on, let's get out of here. The Tavern?"

I shook my head. "No, I'm not in the mood."

She set her bowl on the coffee table, pivoted on the sofa, and took my hand between hers. "You listen to me, Reese Parker, that man loves you. I don't care if he's acting like a fool right now. Maybe they weren't together. Maybe they were just in the same place at the same time. You know how the paparazzi makes things look like something they're not. He's a big story right now." I nodded. "Well, there you go."

"Do you really think that's all it is?"

"Most definitely. And if not, then to hell with him. You're going to the gala of the season with the best date in town." I laughed and she winked. "Everything will be fine. I promise. Look at me, I'm single and love it."

"That's because you don't believe in commitment."

Alexa shook her head. "Yes, I do. I'm committed to us having the best time as we paint the town in pink and black. Oh, and to having more shoes than days in the year."

Once again I laughed at my friend. "What would I do without you?"

She shrugged and picked up her bowl. "Aren't you lucky that you'll never need to find out?"

Nodding, I said, "Yes, I'm the luckiest."

24

Trent

TIME SEEMED TO BE IN a vacuum of sorts. I couldn't believe three weeks had already passed since Sam told me about Phoenix. When the plane landed, beads of sweat immediately dotted my brow, and it wasn't because of the warm desert air. This was a big day for me. One I never thought I'd need to worry about. Maybe that was what made all of this more difficult. Taking things for granted in life whether it be business or personal, wasn't the smartest thing to do. Inevitably, something went wrong. And the building with a flaming bird and not a rocket painted on the facade proved that. The irony of a bird had me shaking my head.

Life had a way of screwing with you when you least expected it. Thanks to Jackson's nickname for

Reese, would I ever be able to look at a feathered creature without thinking of the feisty blonde who made me feel as alive as I did when our team lined up in the red zone? Would I be able to feel the adrenaline pump again through my veins as I stared at the end zone, knowing it was up to me to lead us to get points on the board? To not feel a loss when I didn't step onto the field on game day? If I had to guess, I'd say no.

All of those things had rooted in my soul. The thought of never feeling that exhilaration again forced me to take a step forward. Despite feeling like a rookie rather than a seasoned player, the need to compete trumped my nerves. Sam stood beside me as we walked into the large building. Marble floors with their logo embedded in mosaic tiles in the center of the lobby greeted us. We signed in at the desk and took the elevators to the fifth floor. Jennifer, the second-in-command to the GM for Phoenix, greeted us with a firm handshake as soon as we stepped off the elevator.

"Welcome to Phoenix. It's great to see you both."

"You as well," Sam jovially said, as though we didn't have a care in the world.

I stood with my hands shoved into the front pockets of my pants. Snapping out of it, I forced a smile, and despite the few murmurs from employees in the nearby cubicles dotting the space, I finally spoke, "Yes, thank you so much for having us."

"We're pleased you could make it." We walked down a hallway flanked with framed photos of previous players through the years adorning the walls. "As you know, Trent, you've always been on top our list as the one who got away," Jennifer stated matter-of-factly with a hint of awe in her tone.

Relaxing my shoulders at her statement, allowed me to take a breath I'd been holding. "Thank you. That's nice of you to say."

"It's the truth." She stopped in front of an office door and motioned for us to go inside. "Let's sit and talk." We all sat at a round table in front of a window boasting a view of the city's skyline.

After listening to a bit of the team's history, Sam and Jennifer began negotiations as though I wasn't sitting there. Words like contract, salary, offer, and my move to Arizona were all mentioned. Naturally if I signed on with them there would be a lot of press to deal with and camps I'd need to attend.

By my quick calculations, the annual salary would place me at the third highest paid quarterback in the league. The contract would be for three years contingent on me passing a physical. Jennifer also mentioned they were rebuilding, and I would be a great fit.

Everything sounded perfect. *Then why did it all feel so wrong?*

Sam must have sensed my apprehension and

was most likely nervous I'd flat out decline right then and there. Except I had no desire to do that. Or maybe he thought I'd sign without allowing him the opportunity for *them* to get nervous so he could raise my annual pay and sweeten the deal even more. That was what he did with the Rockets. As soon as they heard their rival, the Thunder, wanted me, they made an offer that rivaled all others—no pun intended.

An hour passed, Jennifer gave us a quick tour of the complex. We stepped outside to look at the practice field. The warm air lifted my hair and it wasn't lost on me how nice that felt in comparison to the East Coast. I supposed that was one of the bonuses if I moved. Spending my senior collegiate year in California to be with my mother, provided me the opportunity to be in a nicer climate. When I wasn't bogged down in pads and equipment, I definitely preferred the heat. That was another plus to moving to Arizona. I'd be closer to my family. On the other hand, I'd be farther away from Reese and Jackson. Unless he came to Arizona.

Out of the fifty plus players on the team's roster, I knew about five of them personally. The others I'd either met after a game or at an event. It had always been important to me to build a comradery with my fellow teammates. I'd miss that in DC. Those guys were like my brothers. A fraternity of sorts without all of the bull that came with pledging.

We stopped in front of one of the fields, and I was immediately hit with the new turf smell that reminded me of a new car. A few guys were at the opposite end getting ready to paint the hashtags and yard lines. I stood and stared for a moment. Even with open eyes I could hear the hard hits of helmets and pads coming together.

"How's the practice squad?"

Jennifer's brows pulled together. "How do you mean?"

"Any standouts?"

Many people didn't know that my go-to wide receiver was once on the Rockets' practice squad. Well, they may have known when he first made an appearance on the active roster, but now he was just a great player who put up points almost every game. To the league, the squad weren't scrubs, they were loaded with potential. A minor league team within a league if you will. We weren't like baseball or hockey that had players we could call up to join us. No, we relied on them.

"A few. None that are ready to move up."

The ego in me wanted to tell her to let me be the judge of that. Instead, I just nodded. If I did choose to move to Phoenix, I'd make sure to assess them myself.

Forty minutes later Sam and I were in the car heading back to the airport. I knew he wanted to talk about everything, but all I wanted to do was relax. My knee reminded me it wasn't fully healed. That had been clear by the dull ache as we walked and stood around a bit too much. Once I got home, I'd ice and elevate it and all would be good.

Clearly he hadn't received my silent memo because he asked, "So, it's a good deal. What do you think?"

"They're in the ballpark."

Sam chuckled. "Do me a favor and think about it. Think about everything from the move to your leg."

I knew he left out Reese's name on purpose. Maybe he could tell she was one thing I couldn't stop thinking about. Would I ever again be responsible for her pretty lips curling up in the corners? Or be the one to bring her extreme pleasure? We'd only been together once and the thought of her sweetness surrounding another man made all of me hurt… not just my leg. All. Of. Me.

Dammit, if only things could be different. Then maybe I wouldn't be driving myself crazy. It would be inevitable for her to find someone to love her. Giving me the finger should have been an indication of where we were heading. I'd never met someone so stubborn in all of my life. Of course, she'd say the same of me. Enemies to lovers… strangers to lovers… friends to non-lovers. Thanks to those sappy movies, all of those tropes ran through my head as Reese explained them. And thanks to those cheesy flicks, I thought maybe we stood a shot. Then again, those were make-believe. In real life, half, if not all, of those couples would be like Reese and me—apart. But they all got their happily ever afters. We only got the after, and so far it sucked.

Leaning my head back, I closed my eyes. I never answered Sam and since he didn't say anything more for the remainder of our flight, he knew not to bring it up. The man had a job to do. Ironically, it was for me and still I couldn't bring myself to think about moving away from DC. Too bad there was a high probability of that happening.

For the next four hours, rather than dwell on the negative things in my life, I let the sounds of the jet's engines lull me to sleep. Maybe when I woke up things would be different. Except the probability of *that* was slim to none.

25

Reese

EVEN THE SMELL OF BUTTER and sugar couldn't pull me out of my funk. Every time the bell above the door sounded, I immediately looked to see if a pair of sexy green eyes would greet me. I don't remember the last time I lay in bed at night and didn't stare at my ceiling. Each night my mind ran through various scenarios of how it would go down when Trent came to see me—because in my dreamy thoughts that was how it would happen.

Except, he hadn't walked in. Customers came and went, a couple reporters popped in that Erica politely sent on their way with a dozen cookies. I would have just kicked them out empty-handed, but she believed her sweet cut-outs only made things better. I suppose that was what made Sugarcoat This! a successful business.

Poor Alexa did everything short of dancing on the tables to change my sour mood—I had no doubt that would be coming if I didn't perk up. "Do you want to go to the Tavern tonight? It's ladies' night. And you know that brings the boys to the bar." I shook my head but couldn't help a small laugh that came out. "See, it'll be good for you. Come on, let's go."

"Maybe."

Alexa beamed. "So much better than a flat-out no. Progress, my dear child." She popped a kiss on my cheek and tossed me a towel. "Who knows, maybe you'll meet someone? You know the best way to get over someone—"

My hand flew up. "I got it, thanks." The bell rang, and my head snapped to the front of the store. A few ladies walked in with shopping bags. Not wanting to look like a teenage girl waiting for her phone to ring... because that hadn't happened either, I made my way around the glass case, and toward the four-top that needed to be cleaned.

Long seconds had drifted by when that damn door opened again. *Don't look,* I told myself. Because another scenario that played in my head was that he would walk in with a bevy of women on his arms. Why wouldn't I think that when I decided to scan the internet for pictures of Trent? Dumb. Dumb. Dumb. Thankfully, none had been too recent, but he definitely never lacked female companionship.

Thinking about the time he called Casey to tell her that we were together should have been a beacon of how desired he'd been. I could only imagine her elation knowing he was now available.

Ugh. *Snap out of it!* I heard Cher scream at me. Maybe I did need to get out more and stop watching movies. And maybe I should have looked the last time the door opened because when I looked up, a tall, dark, and handsome man stood in front of me. Except his eyes weren't the ones I'd been dreaming of. My fingers hadn't played with his hair. And worst of all, he didn't make my heart grow wings and soar.

"Hey, Bird."

"Hi, Jackson…" My voice trailed off as fear told me not to turn around.

"He's not here." I nodded at his flat tone trying not to look disappointed. "Can we sit for a minute?" Jackson pulled a chair out for me, not leaving me a chance to answer. "I want to talk to you about Trent."

"Is he okay?"

A tight smile grew across his handsome face. "Yes, he just got back from Arizona. They made him an offer."

Another inevitable occurrence. "That's good. I'm sure that made him happy."

"So you do still care about him."

I could feel my eyebrows tighten. Almost feeling offended, I didn't know how to respond to that. Then just like when I last saw Trent, my blood began to simmer. "I'm not exactly sure why anyone would think otherwise."

"He told me what happened."

"Right, so this is all my fault?" The legs on my chair screeched across the floor as I stood. "Was there anything else, because I'm working?"

"I didn't come here to upset you."

Annoyed I just shook my head. "I'm sorry, and I don't mean this rudely, but why are you here? It's clear that Trent is ready to move on. In some ways he has, hasn't he?"

"Yeah, I guess, but—"

My hand flew up, stopping him. I couldn't listen to Jackson tell me Trent was back to his whatever ways with Casey. Or worse that he was moving across the country. At least he didn't need to go into hot pursuit to gain her attention. All of my thoughts made my stomach flip. When I glanced up and locked eyes with Alexa, she must have sensed my need to be rescued and tossed me a lifeline.

"Reese, can you give me a hand for a minute?" When Jackson pivoted in his chair she added, "Sorry to interrupt. Hi, Jackson."

"Hey." He stood and the blank look on his face said it all. "I should get going. Good to see you both again."

Jackson took a couple steps forward, stopped, turned, and his lips parted but no words came out. Instead he blandly raised his hand before walking out the door. That damn chime sounded more ominous as the day went on and I still had no idea why he came. However he did confirm my suspicions that Trent had moved on.

Letting out a long exhale, I wrung the small towel between my hands. "Are you okay?" Alexa gave me one look before pulling me into her arms. "Did he say something about Trent?"

"Yeah. He has just come back from a meeting in Arizona. It's fine. I knew he wouldn't listen to me. He's an athlete. Sometimes their need to compete outweighs everything else. As long as he's happy…"

"He's dumb." I couldn't help but chuckle. "He is, Reese. Let's just forget about men for a while. We're going to have the best time at the gala, right?"

"Yes, you're absolutely right. I think we should go to the salon before the event. I could use some highlights."

"That's my girl! Ooh… let's get our makeup done too."

Finally feeling a bit better, I nodded. "Sounds perfect."

Alexa hugged me once more, and I'd never been

more thankful to be able to call her my best friend.

The opulent pink, black, and gold décor looked magical. All the tables in the Opal Hotel's grand ballroom were similarly decorated with a low floral arrangement for easy conversation, black linen table cloths, and alternating pink and white napkins. Just stunning.

Soft music from the six-piece band along with chatter and laughter from the guests filled the room. Alexa and I stood in the doorway, taking it all in. Thanks to my nervousness, we opted to skip the dinner portion of the event and instead grabbed dinner on our own before heading over.

Most of the men had on black tuxedos. Some with pink vests, others with pink ties in either traditional or bow styles. There were a few men who dared to wear a pink tux, which brought a smile to my face. All of the women may as well have walked out of a fashion magazine. It amazed me that despite the number of guests, I hadn't seen any duplicate dresses. Granted, most were full-length and there was probably a seventy/thirty percent split between black and pink, but it seemed I had been the only one to wear a dress that didn't hit the floor.

Of course I couldn't help my wandering eyes from scanning the room in search of familiar faces. I knew my grandparents would be here as well as others from the Thunder's organization. I recognized a few, but still no sign of Trent. I let out a sigh, wondering if maybe that was a good thing. However, when it came to him, I didn't know what was good anymore.

Photographers and local news reporters chatted with some of the benefactors and guests. Every year this event grew in popularity. The tickets carried a hefty price tag that, aside from a very small portion, all went to the *Kids Around the Corner* foundation.

"Hey, let's get a drink." Alexa looped her arm through mine and guided me toward the bar at the side of the room. We stood in line waiting our turn, and once again, my eyes began to wander. That time they landed on my grandmother, who raised her hand before leaning in to say something to my granddad.

"Wow, he's spectacular." Alexa tilted her head in the direction of the very handsome bartender as we inched our way forward. Yes, he was very good-looking, but at the moment all I cared about was if he could mix a cocktail. As always, this event had a list of signature blends, most of which were pink.

"Good evening, ladies. What can I get you?"

Alexa gave him a smile that I'd seen several times before. One that ensured our drinks wouldn't be watered down or made with more mixer than liquor. "I'll have the Party in Your

Mouth." My head snapped toward my best friend as I felt blood fill my face. "What?" she asked incredulously with a shrug before pointing toward a small chalkboard sitting on the corner of the bar. "It's on the menu."

"Oh, right." I shyly smiled. "Make it two please."

When we had our drinks in hand, we turned, intent on going to greet my grandparents. Except they were dancing. A genuine smile spread across my face. There were no two people in the world that I loved more. Since I was a little girl, I'd hoped to find what they had. I continued to stare at them when Kenzie and Dave came into view. She was laughing at something he must have said. Either that or he stepped on her foot—something my sister was used to, according to her.

My *Party in Your Mouth* drink bizarrely tasted like strawberry shortcake mixed with a tartness I couldn't put my finger on. Either way, it was delicious and slid down my throat rather easily as we strolled around the room.

"Girls, you look divine!" Mrs. Lancaster air-kissed our cheeks. "Just lovely. Your dresses suit you both perfectly." Someone called her name and waved. "Please excuse me. Have a good time, ladies."

She glided away in her full-length black gown. "I love her." Alexa beamed, draining her drink. "Want another?"

I knew I shouldn't, but nodded anyway. When

I went to move with her, she shook her head. "I'll get them. You can wait for your grandparents."

The hairs on the back of my neck stood on end as the chill traipsed down my bare arms, causing my skin to prickle. Slowly lifting my gaze, my heart slammed into my throat. For a minute, I thought it had stopped beating, seeing Trent on the dance floor with Casey. Then when his eyes met mine, my pulse quickened and filled my eardrums, muffling out the sounds around me. Including Alexa calling out my name as I ran out of the ballroom, once again leaving a piece of my soul behind.

26

Trent

WHY? WHY DID I DANCE with Casey? All night, I stared at the door, waiting for Reese to show up. When I saw the two vacant chairs at her grandparents' table, I assumed she wouldn't be coming. More than once, I tried to speak to Charles Reese, but each of those times something or someone stopped me. I'd given three interviews, the last with Casey when her "favorite" song came on — or so she said.

Ever since she heard I had been released from the Rockets and that my love life was no longer, Casey took it upon herself to try and cheer me up. She'd send texts with positive quotes, letting me know her shoulder would be available at any time. Things a friend would say to another.

At first, I thought they were texts of genuine

concern. Then they took a personal turn and in no way, shape, or form did I have any intention of using her shoulder or any other part of her, regardless that we'd been *familiar* with each other in the past. Not wanting to lead her on, all of my messages blandly stated her concern was appreciated.

A couple weeks ago, we ran into each other in a café. Connor, the young boy I'd met at the diner before my life went into a complete upheaval, happened to be there with his mom. He had been telling me about his classmates and teacher the day he brought in the hat. How they didn't have a test, thanks to her being in a good mood for a change. The kid had me and the people around us in stitches.

That was when Casey walked up. Connor recognized her from TV and he adorably repeated everything he had just told me to her. We had a great laugh, and that was the end of it. Something about that exchange seemed to give her the wrong impression because before she left, she rolled up on her toes, kissed my cheek, and told me to call her if I couldn't sleep... or anytime. Innocent? Maybe if we didn't have a past.

Tonight had been no different. Like a vulture waiting for its prey, she sauntered up to me in a long black gown that hugged her curves so tightly it was a wonder she could walk without needing to shuffle her feet. Being a former pageant girl, I suspected she was used to it. Even Jackson, who had been at my side all night before Mrs. Lancaster's niece asked him to dance, noticed.

Casey placed her hand on my forearm. "Dance with me?" she asked, batting her eyelashes.

Thinking that would be a great time to let her down gently, we walked onto the parquet floor. She coiled her arms around my neck, while my hand stayed firmly planted on her waist. It felt elementary, stiff, and as unromantic as I could make it. Casey glanced up, and as though the proverbial lightbulb amped up its wattage, she shook her head. "You're in love with her, aren't you?"

Love. Yeah. But no way would she be hearing it before Reese.

"Look Casey, I like you."

An unexpected laugh bubbled out of her. "No need to explain. It's all good, really. I don't know what got into me. I never should have sent you those texts. I'm sorry. You should go after your girl. I'm actually surprised she isn't here."

That was when my eyes saw a vision in pink. Reese looked absolutely breathtaking. Most of the other women's dresses reached their feet and the majority of them were black. Reese Parker once again stood out in a crowd. Except this time when our eyes met, she didn't give me the finger. Instead, I watched the color drain from her face, the corners of her lips that I ached to kiss turn down, and when she spun and bolted out the door, my heart sank.

Not bothering with an explanation or goodbye, I left Casey on the dance floor, intent on making things right with Reese. After avoiding a few people who tried to talk to me, I ran out of the room and down the stairs, ignoring the protest from my knee. Once in the lobby, my eyes quickly scanned the room, but no sign of Reese.

People stood at the check-in desk with their bags near them. Maybe she got a room? But rather than wait in line, I hurried out the front door in hopes I'd find her. The cool evening air did nothing to abate my racing thoughts. I stood on the sidewalk and looked in every direction hoping to spot Reese.

"Pretty girl, pink dress?" A uniformed bellman asked, standing at the valet stand. His gray hair lifted at the end as he hung a set of keys in the box behind him.

"Yes, did you see where she went? Did she look okay?"

"Don't know where she was headed. Don't know much about how she looked except to say, she didn't seem as though she had a very good time tonight. I do know she got in a hired car and went that way." He lifted his hand and pointed to his right.

Either this guy didn't know who I was or didn't care. I ran my hand through my hair. Jackson drove tonight with the idea that I needed to let loose a little. "Can you get me a car, please?"

He stepped onto the sidewalk and waved his hand in the air. In less than thirty seconds, I was in a car heading toward Reese's house in hopes she'd let me explain… and forgive me for stupidly letting her go.

I watched the street lights reflect off the wet asphalt as we rounded the corner. Every so often, I'd see the driver glance at me in his rearview mirror. He looked to be around Reese's age or maybe a bit younger.

"Are you Trent Archer?"

The last thing I wanted was to talk about myself, but it didn't look as though I had much choice. All I wanted was to get to Reese. "Yeah."

"Man, I think you're great. DC is dumb for releasing you. I've seen every one of your games, studied the way you moved, and hoped to get a full ride to a D-one school. Your drop-back in the pocket and quick release were epic… are epic," he amended.

Despite not wanting to talk, I decided to ask, "You're a quarterback?"

He grimly chuckled. "Was, yeah. Busted my back screwing around with my friends during spring break my senior year. Blew my ride. Sucks."

"Sorry, that had to be rough."

"It was. I know you understand because of your

injury, but at least you got to play. I'd give anything to have had even one season in the pros. I wouldn't care if I was on the last place team. To play the sport I loved in front of a crowd of thousands..." He paused and stopped at a red light. "What a rush."

A rush. The kid was right. Stepping onto the field in a professional stadium was more than I ever imagined it would be. "What's your name?"

"Joe. Joe Bevins." I searched my memory, trying to remember if I heard his name or not, but it didn't ring a bell. "Grew up in North Carolina... Navy brat," he continued. "My mom got transferred to DC and since I didn't have much going on, I moved up here with my parents. This driving gig is until I find something else." Brake lights in front of us seemed amplified thanks to the cloud-covered moon. When the car slowed, I sat up straighter in my seat. "Looks like an accident up ahead."

Blue and red lights flashed, sirens sounded, and a police officer stood in the road directing traffic around the crash. As we slowly drove by I turned my head and saw a pouf of pink standing near an ambulance.

"Stop the car." I hurriedly fished a hundred dollar bill out of my wallet, handed it to him, and hopped out before rushing toward the crash. Glass crunched under my dress shoes as I looked at the banged up sedan and a pickup truck that sustained the hit better than the car had.

An officer tried to stop me, but for once I was glad to be recognized. "That's my girlfriend," I shouted above the commotion and pointed toward the ambulance pulled off to the side with its back doors open.

When he stepped aside, I rushed forward, only to halt five feet away from her. A woman in a blue uniform stood in front of her, waving a small flashlight into Reese's eyes. I felt my heart dip at the thought of something happening to her, especially with us being on the outs.

Taking a couple steps forward to close the gap, I heard the EMT say, "You may have a small concussion." Reese nodded, looking as though she'd been crying. What killed me was I had no idea if the tears were for what she'd seen or the accident. "Is there someone you can call? You should be fine to go home. If not, we can take you to Memorial."

Startling both of them, I blurted, "I'll take her."

Reese's lip started to quiver and not waiting for permission, I went to her, pulled her into my arms, and let her cry against my chest. Her hands working their way onto my spine had me tightening my hold. If anything would have happened to her, forgiving myself would have been impossible. It was my fault she rushed out of the gala. It was my fault we hadn't been together. It was my fault this beautiful woman was hurt.

"Miss?" I gently stroked Reese's back, loosened my hold, and kissed the top of her head before looking at the EMT. "Will you be okay with him taking you or would you like to come with us?"

"Let me take you home, Reese. I'm so sorry for everything." She gave an assuring nod to let the EMT know that was the plan. Ironically, the woman began to explain concussion protocol to me, handed me a packet of instructions, and Reese's small purse.

"Thank you, I'll take good care of her." That was when I realized I hadn't driven. Glancing around, Joe stood off to the side. Thankfully, he had the common sense to pull over and wait.

I took Reese's hand and helped her down. She looked around and gasped when she saw the car she had come in. "Is the driver okay?"

"Should be fine, miss. A few bumps and bruises."

"Oh, that's good." She began to tremble. I replaced the silver blanket the emergency tech must have given her with my suit jacket. Her gaze lifted to meet mine. "Thank you."

"Come on, let's get out of here."

Rather than lace my fingers with hers, I bent over, slid my arm beneath her legs, keeping my other on her back, and picked her up.

"Your knee…" she whispered.

"I'm fine, Reese." Without further protest, she rested her head on my chest and allowed me to carry her to the car.

Joe stood at the side and, as soon we approached him, opened the back door.

"Thank you."

Poor kid's voice quivered. "Is she okay?"

Reese raised her head. "Hi. I'll be fine."

Joe's eyes widened and in the ambient light I could see his face blush. He glanced up and a small smile tickled his lips. Then it dawned on me that he recognized who she was. Joe confirmed it when he said, "Glad to hear that, Miss Parker."

As carefully as I could, I set her down on the backseat, placed the small purse on her lap, and tucked the pink skirt of her dress inside so I could close the door before walking to the other side. Joe and I both got in, I gave him her address, and he pulled onto the road.

Other than the sound of tires on the wet asphalt, silence filled the car. Sitting next to her without touching her was impossible, so I did. Tentatively but with purpose, I reached for her hand resting on her lap and took it in mine.

Reese stared at where we were joined before looking up at me. Sadness, confusion, and an indescribable emotion tugged at my heartstrings. There were so many things I needed to say to her. Her fingers flexed between mine. I dropped my head, lifted her hand, kissed it, and whispered, "I'm so sorry," against her cool skin.

Twenty or so minutes later, we were at her

home, standing in her living room. She yawned, turned, and gave me a puzzled look.

"What's wrong? Do you feel dizzy? Do you have a headache?"

She blinked a few times. "No. I mean, yes, my head hurts a little, but I'm wondering why you aren't at the gala? When I left—"

"Not now." Once again with her hand in mine, I led her up the stairs to her room. "Let's get you comfortable, then we can talk."

She pivoted on her sexy as sin shoes. "Can you unzip me please?"

Swallowing because Reese suddenly seemed small and fragile, I lifted the small tab and lowered it until the teeth separated and her back was exposed.

"Thank you. I'm going to change. I'll be back."

Rather than do that in front of me, Reese held her dress against her chest, assuring it wouldn't slip, grabbed a pair of pajamas she had atop her bed, and went into the bathroom. Before the door closed, I told her I'd be waiting for her.

When the soft click sounded, I stripped out of my jacket, shirt, and tie, leaving me in my suit pants and white T-shirt. Normally, I slept in boxers, but not wanting to make her uncomfortable or create an awkward situation, I decided that wasn't a banner idea.

Assuming her grandparents would be worried about her, I sent Charles a quick text, letting him know what happened and that I was with Reese. Naturally, he wanted to come over, but he knew she'd need rest. He thanked me and said he'd tell Alexa.

A few minutes passed before the door opened, but it felt like an eternity. When Reese finally stepped out, her hair was down and her face was devoid of any makeup, including the black streaks her tears had created. She set her dress on the chair in the corner of the room, and placed her shoes under it. When she turned, her confused focus was first on her bed before she directed it toward me.

"I need to monitor you. I know enough about concussions to know what to do. If it makes you uncomfortable, I'll be more than happy to sleep in the chair."

"No, that won't be necessary." She lifted the covers and slid beneath them. I lay down next to her and rolled to my side to face her.

"Can I get you anything?"

"I'm fine, really, but thank you." I adjusted the pillow behind me, doing my best not to jostle the mattress too much. "Trent?"

"Hmm…"

"Why aren't you at the gala? Before I left, I saw you… dancing… with Casey."

God, I was such an idiot. "What you saw was Casey finally realizing there would never be anything romantic between us. When you left, I followed. Just not quick enough."

"But I saw you together on the news. You were at the café together and from what I could tell, it looked as though you were having a good time."

She looked so tired, but I knew she should stay awake just a little longer thanks to the knock on her head. "Yes, Casey and I happened to be at the café at the same time. Connor, the kid I told you about from the diner, was there. His stories about school the day he met me made us all laugh. Did you honestly think I would immediately hook up with someone?"

When her pretty eyes lowered, I reached forward to cup her cheek. "Let's talk about this in the morning. It's been a long night."

"Okay, you're going to be here when I wake up, right?"

Thinking back to that fateful day when everything careened downhill, my chest filled with guilt. Seeing that car, then Reese by that ambulance, scared me to death. It made me realize she may have felt that way after my injury. I brought my lips to her forehead and kissed her.

"I promise you, I'm not going anywhere."

Reese closed her eyes. I turned off the light on the bedside table and set my phone's alarm to remind me to check on her in an hour. Resting my head on the pillow, I stared at the ceiling, silently thanking God that she was okay.

27

Reese

SUNLIGHT BREACHING THE WINDOW SHADES stunned my pupils as I tried to open my eyes. Everything around me felt out of sorts. Memories of hydroplaning, crunching metal, the loud pop of the driver's airbag, and the smell of burned fabric from its deployment, all came rushing back to me. As did the memory of Trent appearing seemingly out of nowhere.

That was when I remembered he brought me home. For a moment, or several moments throughout the night, I imagined Trent by my side. But when I heard a faint snore, I knew it wasn't my mind playing tricks on me. Trent was in my bed asleep next to me.

Our conversation from the night before played in my head. I was thankful he wasn't with Casey, an emotion that made me feel a bit better, but there was still the matter of his career. We'd never see eye-to-eye about it. If he moved somewhere to play, how could I possibly cheer him on? My eyes rolled at my own thoughts. Trent wasn't my boyfriend, despite how lovingly he acted last night.

He blinked a few times before blessing me with those beautiful green eyes I'd missed so much.

"Good morning. How are you feeling?"

"A little sore, but other than that I feel fine."

Trent sat up, the covers fell away, and his bare chest looked more toned than I remembered. Staring seemed to be the only option because that was what I did.

"Sorry, I got warm last night." He got out of bed, reached for his T-shirt, and slid it on. Every one of his abs flexed in his movements. "Can I get you anything? Coffee? I'll make us breakfast."

Taking his lead, I pushed the covers off, and when I stood a rush of reality slammed into me. "Thank you for taking care of me. I could use a cup of coffee."

He ran his fingers through his sexy bedhead hair before coming to stand in front of me. "Reese, last night scared the hell out of me." Not knowing what to say other than, *how do you think I felt when I saw you hit the turf and get carted off,* I remained silent. Trent reached forward and cupped my cheek. It took every bit of resolve not to lean into it.

"How did you find me? My purse had been thrown off of my lap, and I didn't have my phone to call anyone." My eyes sprung wide while my heart dropped. "Oh no! Alexa and my grandparents. I never called them."

"I took care of it. I sent your grandfather a text last night when you were in the bathroom. He said he'd tell Alexa. You should probably call them a little later."

"Okay, thank you for doing that."

"I'd do anything for you, Reese." Not wanting to delve into all the meaning of that comment, I remained silent. "Come on, let's go eat."

Trent on the football field was sexy. Trent naked was amazing. Trent cooking? Well, that took his amazing sexiness to an entirely different level. I sat at my kitchen island, while he stood in front of the stove making pancakes. It didn't matter that he had a dress shirt on, each muscle in his back could still be seen.

A circle flew into the air before it landed on a plate. I took a sip of my orange juice just as he placed a small stack of hotcakes in front of me.

"I hope you don't mind, I found a mix in your cabinet and figured I couldn't screw them up."

"Mind? Are you kidding?" I drizzled syrup over the top, cut into them, and slid a forkful into my mouth. "So good," I mumbled between chews. Before I knew it, half of them were gone.

Trent placed his hands on his side of the counter, leaned forward, and locked eyes with me. "I'm really sorry for what I said to you at your grandfather's office. Everything spiraled quickly. When I heard you tell him you wouldn't want me on the Thunder, something inside of me broke, and I snapped."

I dabbed my lips with a napkin. He thinks something inside of him broke? My heart shattered that day. Still, staying angry wouldn't help matters. According to Jackson, Trent had moved on. Since it hadn't been with Casey, it must mean he would be joining another team.

"I'd say the same, but I'm not sorry. Granddad asked me for my opinion, and I gave it. I'd give the exact advice again. My mind won't change." His Adam's apple worked down a hard swallow. "I know that isn't what you want to hear, but it's the truth." Taking a moment to collect my thoughts, having an internal debate as to whether or not I wanted to know, I added, "Jackson told me you went to Arizona to talk to them."

"I did. They made me an offer."

Forcing a smile, I rolled my shoulders back. "You need to do what makes you happy. Not me, your fans, or an eager organization. It's your life and you should live it how you'd be happiest."

"What about you?"

"Me? Well, if we're being honest, you said hearing my words at Grandad's office caused something inside of you to break. Watching you walk away from me that day crushed me. It almost made me wish I still hated you."

"Why?"

"Because hating you was easier than loving and losing you."

His head dropped forward and hung between his shoulders. Not knowing what to do, I slid off the stool. The cool hardwood beneath my bare feet did little to ebb the heat rising up my spine.

"I don't know how to respond to that." Trent finally raised his head and his green eyes shimmered with sadness. "Somewhere along the line or maybe it was the day in the stadium, I fell for you, Reese. But I understand where you're coming from. The last thing I'd ever want is to make your life difficult."

One tear slid from each of my eyes. "Looks like we're at a crossroads."

Trent strode around the island until he was next to me. He took my cheeks in his hands, ran his thumbs along the damp path on my skin, and brought his lips to mine. It wasn't a sexual kiss or a kiss that said we can get through this. It was a kiss that felt like goodbye. My arms lopped around his neck, forcing his hands to move to my hips. Our bodies pressed against one another as we held each other for what I believed was the last time.

Breaking apart, I used his move and cupped his stubbled cheek with my hand. *I love you* tickled the tip of my tongue but those three words never came out. The ache in my chest was palpable. At one point, I wondered if he could hear it breaking.

"I should get going." Trent took a step back and my hand limply fell to my side. "Be sure not to push yourself today." When I arched a brow, his lips quirked to the side. "Just take it easy."

"Okay."

We walked toward my front door and each step felt longer than the last.

"Thanks again, Trent."

Trent kissed my cheek before walking out the door and most likely out of my life.

28
Trent

BEADS OF SWEAT ROLLED DOWN my spine as I completed my fourth mile on the elliptical. I had a meeting in an hour with Sam, but all I thought about was when I was at Reese's house. That night, all I could do was stare at her. Setting my alarm for every hour to wake her and ensure she was okay was futile; I couldn't sleep anyway. Each time I closed my eyes, I pictured her and that ambulance and gripping fear enveloped me.

Over and over I replayed our conversation after my meeting with her grandfather. *"Do you know how terrifying that is to me? To everyone who loves you? So you can think what you want, but it's because of how much I care that I can't be the one responsible. I'm sorry."*

My legs slowed, and I reached forward to end

my workout then stepped off the machine. As though lightning had struck, I knew what I had to do. Sam may not be thrilled with my choice, but I had a feeling he'd understand. If not, too bad because I needed to do what was best for me and for Reese.

Filled with a bit more hope and a lot of adrenaline, I skipped icing my knee and headed straight to my room for a shower. Everyone I cared about popped into my head as my thoughts once again began to bounce around. Usually, when I felt this hyped, it had to do with a new play I wanted to try at practice. Sometimes the coach liked it and other times he said trick plays were for the weak. In my opinion, they were the opposite. It took a set of brass ones to pull off any sort of out-of-the-box move when a line of bulky men wanted to crush you… and believe me, I knew that better than most.

Today, the play that came to mind had nothing to do with being on the field — not directly anyway. It was also not for the weak because in about an hour, I planned on telling Sam I was done playing. The second part of my idea hitched on Charles and his stunning granddaughter.

Not wanting to delay my future any more than I already had, I turned off the water, dried off, got dressed, and grabbed my keys.

"Call Sam Jasper," I said to my car's Bluetooth as I pulled out of my driveway.

"Good morning," he answered with an upbeat tone that only he would have on a Monday morning.

"Hey, Sam. I have a change of plans." His exhale rang loudly through my speakers. "I'll fill you in later, but I need to cancel our meeting. And tell Phoenix I'm not interested."

"Wait… what? You're turning down their offer? I'm not sure we'll get a better one."

"Yes, I'm turning it down. I'm turning all of them down."

"Trent, as your agent, I think you need to tell me what your *plan* is."

"I will, I promise. First, I need to go see a man about a job." Not giving him a chance to ask me any other questions but before I disconnected the call, I said, "Thanks for everything, Sam." Feeling lighter but still nervous, I took the road that led to the Thunder's offices, hoping Charles had time to see me.

After sitting in traffic for close to thirty minutes, rehearsing what I would say to Reese's grandfather, I finally pulled into their parking lot and made my way into the building. A woman stood in front of the elevator bay, and when she turned, her eyes widened.

"Good morning, Kenzie."

"Trent? What are you doing here?"

Not wanting to discuss it in the lobby, I was

thankful when the elevator doors opened. Motioning my hand forward, she stepped in. Nerves started to tickle my pulse. Kenzie pushed the button to the executive's floor, exactly where I was headed, and turned to me.

"Thank you for helping my sister on Saturday. And I'm sorry for sounding rude a moment ago, but you caught me off guard."

"No apologies necessary. As far as your sister is concerned, I'd do anything for her. That's partly why I'm here to speak to your grandfather." There were two things I wanted to talk to him about, one was business, the other personal.

"I'm on my way to see him now, we have a meeting. I assume he doesn't know you are coming?"

"No, he doesn't. I don't want to take up your meeting time but if I could just get a few minutes. Actually, if you could be there, that would be great."

Her eyes narrowed slightly, probably wondering what I was up to. And curiosity must have gotten the best of her because it hadn't taken long for her to say, "I look forward to whatever it is you need to talk to my grandfather about."

"Thanks, Kenzie. Reese isn't here today is she?"

"Not that I'm aware of."

The chime sounded right before the chrome doors slid open. We made our way down the hallway that I now noticed was a bit different than the one in Phoenix. Yes, there were pictures of previous players on the wall, but mostly the pictures were of Charles and his family. I stopped at one where he was standing on the team's logo on the fifty yard line with two young girls by his side. The dark-haired one smiled at the camera, the blonde, who appeared to be about five years old, looked up at Charles.

"That's Reese and me," Kenzie said with a laugh. "Not that you couldn't tell. That was right before Opening Day. I'll never forget how Reese took everything in. Even as a kid she's loved this team. Rather than hanging out with her friends, she wanted to be with our granddad. She always had something to say about the game, and to be honest, most of the time she was spot on. That's the thing when it comes to my little sister, when she loves something all she wants is what's best for it."

I nodded. "That's what I love about her... well, one of the things."

A huge smile split her face in two. "I'm glad to hear it."

We turned the corner and walked down the hall to where Reese and I had our misunderstanding. Needing to right it, I stepped into Charles's office. When he looked up, most likely only expecting Kenzie, she explained, "Trent would like a word with us."

The man stood and despite having several conversations with him in the past, it dawned on me the last time I was in this building, I ended up hurting his granddaughter. Ironically, that was about a job too, but this was different.

I extended my hand, which he took and gave a firm shake. "My apologies for barging in. There's something important I'd like to speak to you about. However, before I begin, I want you both to know that if you need to consult with Reese or get her opinion, please do. After all, most of this has to do with her."

"Well, now you've piqued my interest," Charles said, steepling his fingers beneath his chin. "Please have a seat and tell us what brings you here today."

I sat in one of the chairs in front of his desk and Kenzie sat next to me. Feeling nervous, I cleared my throat. "I've decided to retire."

Charles shifted forward. "Rumor had it that many teams were looking at you. From what I understand, Phoenix made you an offer." Leaning a bit closer, he studied me for a long moment. "Is it your health?"

Even without disclosing any personal information, there had been no doubt in my mind that Reese had planted that seed. "Partly, sir. When I saw Reese sitting at the back of that ambulance, everything seemed to come to a sudden halt. The last time I felt crippling fear was when my mother told me she had cancer." His lips turned down. "She's fine now, in remission."

"That's wonderful," Kenzie said, angling her body my way.

"Thank you. It was a major relief for our family. Anyway, seeing Reese like that was a wake-up call I hadn't expected… or quite frankly known I'd needed. It got me thinking that maybe I could still be on a team and not play." Neither Charles nor Kenzie said anything. All my rehearsed lines flew out the window. Beating around the bush had never been my style. "And I was wondering… hoping actually, that you'd consider me for a position on your staff. I happened to hear you might be in need of an assistant offensive coordinator."

Charles's leather chair creaked as he leaned back in it. "Does Reese know you're here?"

"No, sir. I didn't want to involve her. Plus, I have something else to ask of you." I looked at Kenzie. "You too."

"Okay," she said, pulling her eyebrows together much like her sister did when she was confused or intrigued.

"Actually, before you tell me your answer, please know it has no bearing on what else I need to ask you."

Charles chuckled. "Trent, please relax. First, how are you feeling?"

"I'm fine, thank you for asking. Every now and then, I get a small pain, but I'm getting stronger every day."

"I'm glad, that was an awful hit. The owners are actually meeting about rules next month for auxiliary games. Come to think of it, you'd be good to speak to about that before I go."

"Anything you need, sir."

"Right, now about the job. The position of assistant offensive coordinator has been filled as of last Friday. We planned on announcing it later today." Disappointment hit hard until he added, "However, because we promoted internally, we do need a quarterback coach. We're looking for someone dedicated, not afraid of taking risks, and who will be able to help develop the skills, both physically and mentally that are necessary to win."

My gaze went to Kenzie, who nodded. "I'd love a chance to interview for that position. There are many things I could teach them. I know I'm young, but you don't need my résumé to know what I could bring to the organization."

"No, we don't. Now, before we kick you out and talk about you behind your back, what else did you need to ask us?"

Deciding it'd be best to be a bit more formal, I stood, took a step back, and looked at two of the most important people in Reese's life. The only one missing was her grandmother. "I'm in love with Reese." A smile spread across Kenzie's face, giving me the guts to continue. "I'd like to ask her to marry me. Maybe not right now, but soon. I know this may be happening quickly, and if you don't think it's the right time, I'll wait." A little voice inside my head yelled at me for lying. "Actually, that isn't true."

They both laughed. "Does she know how you feel?" Charles asked.

"No sir. She doesn't even know I'm giving up playing."

He got up and walked around his desk until he was standing in front of me. "Welcome to the family, Trent."

"First she needs to say yes."

"Let me rephrase, welcome to the Thunder family. What my youngest granddaughter decides is up to her. But I believe I speak for the both of us that you have our blessing."

"Thank you, sir. Thanks to both of you. I shook their hands and then added, "I just need one more favor."

Reese

EVER SINCE TRENT LEFT MY house a week ago, I'd been aching for him. I'd gotten used to seeing either him or Jackson come into the bakery, but neither had been in. So many times I picked up the phone to call him, but what good would that do? We were no longer together. Except, my heart didn't know that. Nor did my body when I thought about him or heard his name on the news.

Then there was my family. I had no idea what had gotten into them. They'd all been acting so weird lately. Granddad had been evasive, my sister barely spoke more than ten words to me, and my brother-in-law had been MIA. The only normal one, other than Bubba, had been my grandmother. Except when I asked her why all of our family members were acting strangely, she didn't think they were.

Maybe I was the strange one.

To say my life had done a complete 180 since the day I flipped Trent off would be an understatement. As soon as I thought we may have gone full circle, the line broke and the momentum stopped. Maybe starting something with a negative reaction may had set the stage. Except I hadn't planned to start anything. That day in the stands felt liberating, despite being annoying. But, come to find out, that has been true about my relationship with Trent.

Each time I thought *maybe* we'd see eye-to-eye on something important, we didn't, aside from the misunderstanding years ago, which I apologized for. The common denominator in our demise pre and post our friendship had been football. Yes, I may have been biased on wanting him to be with the Thunder. It had been made clear that my granddad didn't hold that animosity. Still, my granddad wasn't looking in the mirror when he got the news that Trent turned him down. I saw the devastation in the lines on his face.

I let out a sigh and rummaged through my cupboards for a snack. Settling on a chewy granola bar and a bottle of water from Iceland, I snagged my laptop and pulled up scouting films I needed to look over. As I watched a few defensive players who definitely ate more than snack bars and water, and some quarterbacks—of course—none compared to the one who had taken residence in my mind and heart. Not that it was fair to compare these kids to Trent, because it wasn't.

Why did I let myself fall? Because he's a good guy. After giving my head a shake, I said out loud, "Great. Now you're talking to yourself." Closing and opening my eyes a few times, I stared at the screen, but after a few seconds, everything blurred. It was no use. Accepting that Trent would be in my thoughts until I purged him, I closed the lid to my computer and tossed it aside.

Alexa told me on more than one occasion that the heart was one of the strongest and weakest muscles in the body. Of course, that description usually came after one of her quick relationships. She wasn't the type to settle down or commit to a guy, but she did commit to herself. My best friend knew what made her happy, and she went for it.

What made me happy? There were a lot of things if I stopped to think about it long enough. No, that wasn't true. I didn't need to stop and think because the answers were simple: my family, friends, and on most days, Trent. Cher as her character from *Moonstruck* once again popped into my head and virtually slapped me... seriously, the woman's hand had to sting by now. Laughing at my dumb imagination, I decided to put on my big girl panties and make a few changes in my life.

The first was my job. As much as I loved working at the bakery, cookies weren't my passion — football, or more precisely, the Thunder was. Not wanting to waste another minute, I hurried and stripped out of my sweats — that were sure to be able to walk on their own soon — showered, and put on my favorite jeans and a T-shirt. Thanks to the spring-weather tease outside, I added my navy and white quarter-zip with the team's logo on my chest. Rather than waste time with my hair, I tossed it into a high ponytail and quickly applied some makeup.

Feeling more presentable than I had in a while, I grabbed my keys and headed toward Granddad's office to see a man about a job.

On my way, my phone dinged with a message from my sister. Hitting the play button on my Bluetooth, the message read,

> *Turn on SportsToday at three p.m.*
> *There's something you need to see.*

I would have replied, but it was almost that time now. If I hurried inside, I could watch it there or better yet, she could tell me why.

As soon as I pulled into the parking lot, I noticed a flurry of activity. At first I thought I may have missed an email, but when I grabbed my phone and checked, nothing popped up to warrant the number of cars and news vehicles. Had granddad signed someone? No, he wouldn't have without telling me.

Then it hit me. Trent. No way would he have signed him after what I had said. Unless the smooth-talker did just that... talked his way into a contract. Frustrated, I hustled out of my car, ignoring a few people calling my name, and ran straight into the lobby, intent on going to my granddad's office, but when I saw people standing outside the pressroom, my feet carried me there instead.

Reporters dictated into their phones, news photographers snapped pictures, and then a reporter said his name — Trent Archer. Unbelievable.

Dipping my head to shield my face, I bypassed the throng of eager beavers waiting to share whatever story lay behind the double doors, and turned right to head down the hall to the back door of the room. After punching in the five-digit code, the lock released with a beep.

I could barely hear anything beyond my pulse drumming in my ears. Then again, I didn't need to, because sitting at the table with microphones in front of them were none other than my granddad and Trent. Annoyed, I scurried and situated myself directly in front of them. In mere minutes this room would be filled with reporters, but right now, I needed answers.

When they looked up, their eyes sprung wide. Well, Trent's did. My granddad had a sweet smile on his face—why that was, I had no idea. Clearly everyone had lost their minds. Then Kenzie came out with a piece of paper in her hand and handed it to Trent. When she caught on that they were staring straight ahead, her eyes followed their sightline.

"Hey, sis. What are you doing here?"

"What am I doing here? How about someone tells me what's going on."

"Trent's joining the team," my granddad gleefully stated as though it would explain everything.

"What?" Turning my attention to Trent, I cocked a brow and he gave me that smile. Damn, he was beautiful. Part of me wanted to cry for how much I missed him. The other part wanted to throttle him for willing to risk his health for a sport.

"We wanted to surprise you. Well, I did," Trent offered as an explanation. "How did you find out?"

"I didn't." Turning my attention to my granddad, I saw joy in his eyes. Despite knowing this could all go badly, I said what I went there to say. "I'm here because... well, to talk to my granddad about something."

Thankfully, he knew better, got up, and came to stand beside me. "What is it, sweetheart?"

Turning my back to Trent and inadvertently my tight-lipped sister, I confessed my reason for being there. "I decided to work for the team." Before I could even utter one more word, my grandfather enveloped me in a hug, just as the main doors opened, and the buzz of eager reporters filled the room.

"I'm so happy," he said, kissing me on the cheek. "We'll talk after. Wow, what a great day this is." Wrinkles jutted out from the outside corners of his eyes and around his lips. The man had gone through a lot over the years and had devoted his life to his family... both blood and team. Because that was what the Thunder was to him... family.

My hand landed on his arm as he turned away from me. "Wait, what is going on here?"

"I don't have time to explain. The doors have opened. Do you trust me?"

I nodded. "Of course I do."

He kissed my cheek and walked back to the table where he took his seat next to Trent and flicked on his microphone. "Thank you for coming today. I know you're all speculating why we called this press conference."

"Is Archer your new QB?" a man shouted from the far side of the room. *That's what I want to know.* Camera shutters mimicked rapid fire around the room as others touted their speculations out loud.

Granddad raised and lowered his right hand, calming everyone down. "Trent, why don't you go ahead and take it from here."

Trent reached forward and slid the silver microphone closer. He cleared his throat and if I hadn't been standing so close to the table, I might have missed his eyes glossing over. "Thank you, Charles." He took a deep breath and tightly grinned. "I'm here to announce my retirement from the sport I love. Football has been the cornerstone of my life for as long as I can remember. But someone very close sent me a bit of a wake-up call." I half-expected him to look at me, but he kept his eyes focused straight ahead as though he'd locked in on a speck on the far wall.

"The injury I sustained in Arizona, did a number on my knee. And although I could eventually play again, I'm making the choice not to. Now, you may be wondering why I'm making this announcement here, at the Thunder's facility..." Yes, that was exactly what I was thinking. "Thanks in part to that person I mentioned earlier, and to the kind man next to me who happens to be her grandfather, I've taken on the role as the Thunder's quarterback coach."

What? My eyes stayed tethered on the pair, who looked as though Santa had just brought them their favorite toy. Even my sister smiled from ear to ear before nodding to me.

Those gorgeous green eyes I'd missed so much

locked with mine. Much like Bubba, I tilted my head and replayed the announcement in my head. He gave one nod and winked before addressing the crowd.

"I'll take one question, then I have a meeting to attend." Trent's deep, sexy voice had a grit to it that made my body thrum with anticipation.

Veronica Tate, the reporter who seemed more interested in gossip than football, stepped forward. Odd that he pointed to her of all people. Then she asked, "What about your relationship with Reese Parker. Rumor has it, you broke up."

Several reporters rolled their eyes while others shouted what a ridiculous question that had been. Trent leaned into the mic. "That's a great question, Ms. Tate." He flipped his attention to me. "Reese, can you come here please?"

I took a deep breath, not knowing what he was about to do, but because I'd been so wrong about things up until now, I did what he asked.

Trent stood and took my hands in his. Once again our eyes locked. "Reese, I'm sorry. When you were in the accident I'd never been so terrified. Well, that was until I thought I could lose you forever. All I ever wanted was to play football, and you're right, I did that. Life, fate, or whatever decided my career was over, but my heart decided we're not. I don't think we'll ever be because, Reese Parker, I love you."

Tears pressed behind my eyes. "You love me?"

"Deeply, madly—" He stopped to kiss the corner of my mouth before whispering in my ear. "Forever. Please tell me I haven't lost you."

His scruff grazed my cheek as he pulled back to study my expression. "You could never lose me."

Cheers from the reporters filled the room when Trent lowered his mouth to mine and kissed me as if we were alone. My entire body hummed with need.

"Ready to get out of here?" I nodded and took a step back before he tugged me to him. "Wait, did you know about this?"

"My granddad called me and asked me to come, but I planned to anyway."

"Why?"

"Because you're looking at the newest member of the Thunder's staff."

Trent lifted me off the ground and spun me around. Reporters started shouting more questions, but when he set me down, he linked his fingers with mine. "Let's go."

I didn't bother to ask where or even say goodbye to my family. We rushed out of the building, into the parking lot, and lights flashed on a Range Rover. He opened the passenger side door, and not caring that my car was there, I got in and buckled up. Half-thinking we'd be going to his house because it was closer than mine, he pulled into the hotel down the road and I sat there for a moment.

"I don't know about you, but I don't feel like

dealing with traffic right now."

"Sounds good to me."

He reached behind his seat and grabbed a navy wool beanie and a pair of glasses. I almost laughed at the thick black rims, but he looked ridiculously handsome in them. Then, he opened his glove compartment and handed me a non-descript baseball cap. "Trust me, you'll want to wear that."

"Okay," I said, sliding it on and pulling my ponytail through the hole in the back. Giving him my attention once more, I couldn't stop my lips from rolling between my teeth.

"What's that look for? It's the glasses, right? Nerd alert is better than jock alert."

"You're wrong. They're beyond sexy. As a matter of fact, when we get into our room, I think you should leave them on."

"Okay, that's it," he barked, getting out of the car and rushing around to open my door. "If we don't hurry, I'm going to be walking with a limp for a reason other than my knee."

I giggled. "Well then, what are we waiting for?"

With purposeful strides and the quickest check-in, we were in our room within minutes.

"I love you, Reese Parker."

"I love you too, Trent Archer. But a little less talk, yes?"

"You know, I'm all about the action."

"Thank God."

Trent

IF YOU COULD GET ME his number, I'd appreciate it."

"Yes, sir," my assistant said right before Reese walked in.

Damn, she was beautiful. Seeing her at work, wearing a sleek dress despite the dress code being casual, spiked my adrenaline.

"Whose number?" she asked, taking a seat on my lap. She crossed her legs, the hem of her dress rose, and my hand rested on the top of her right thigh.

"Joe Bevins." Her brows furrowed. "My driver the night you were in that accident." That memory still haunted me. Leaning forward, I closed the distance between us and kissed her.

"Right, right. I'm sorry, I forgot his name. Why are you calling him? Going somewhere?"

"Not without you I'm not. He told me he used to play and got hurt. Smart guy too, studied all of my films." Reese rolled her eyes, and I laughed. "I want to add him to the staff. The kid loves the sport and not playing has to be rough. This would get him on the field and something tells me the kid is smart."

"Because he watched your films?" She teased with a smirk.

"Yes, exactly."

"Well, I think it's great. We both must have had the same idea because I have Graham Easton coming in tomorrow."

"The kid who wanted the internship?"

"Yes."

"Look at us making dreams come true."

A knock on my door had Reese wanting to get up, but my hand stayed firmly in place. My assistant, Mark, walked in, not at all surprised to see Reese on my lap.

"Sorry to interrupt, but here is Mr. Bevin's number." He handed me a pink slip of paper. "Also, Jackson is waiting to see you."

"Perfect, send him in."

"Can I get up now?"

"No." I chuckled, moving my other hand to her hip.

Jackson strolled in, hands in the front pockets of his pants, his high-top sneaks loosened at the top, and a gray hoodie. To say the man looked relaxed would be an understatement.

"You two should get a room." Reese pushed off me and fixed her dress. "Hey, Bird."

"Hi, Jackson. How are negotiations?"

He shrugged. "Who knows? Every time I call my agent, he tells me to have patience."

Ever since I announced my retirement and new position with the Thunder, my main goal was to get Jackson on this team. Between my coaching and his on-field talent, I had a feeling we'd be unstoppable. Except the Rockets weren't interested in releasing him before his contract expired next year. In fact, they wanted to extend it immediately. Of course, I countered with the sweetest deal Charles and Reese would allow. Giving up draft picks was part of the trade game, but giving up the best ones was team suicide.

"Look, if we can't get you this year, we'll grab you next." Reese's calm voice didn't seem to have the same effect on Jackson because all he did was rake his hand through his hair and groan.

"Yeah. Thanks, I appreciate that."

"Well, I have a meeting to get to." Reese gave Jackson a kiss on the cheek before turning toward me. "I'll see you later."

Before she could take one more step, I snagged

her hand and yanked her against me. Cupping her face, I kissed her. Jackson cleared his throat, but I ignored him. Reese placed her hands on my chest and gently pushed me away before walking out.

"I never thought the day would come," my best friend said, beaming as though he'd solved world hunger.

"What's that?"

"You. The only time I've seen you like this was when we won the championship. I'm happy for you." Jackson's phone rang. He looked at the screen and let out a long breath. "I need to head out. My agent wants to see me. That tells me it isn't going our way. I'll catch you later."

We shook hands and gave each other a one-armed hug. "It'll work out." He raised his hand as he walked out the door.

Before leaving for the day, I called Joe, who couldn't have been more surprised or grateful. He agreed to come in and talk about the job. Truthfully, I think if I told him I wanted him to drive the player cart, he'd do that just to get on the field again. Little did he know what I had in mind was a thousand times better than that. Who better to assist me other than someone who understood the game?

I spent the rest of the afternoon making calls and plans for Reese and me. It seemed that somewhere along the line we missed Valentine's Day. Tonight, I planned on making up for that. She never mentioned it, but when I was in Kenzie's office for a meeting, I couldn't help but notice a card with hearts all over the front of it sitting on her credenza.

Reese thankfully had a meeting, which would give me enough time to get everything ready at my house. Lily, God bless her, picked up the flowers I ordered and placed them around my family room. She also prepared her delicious lasagna that was warming in the oven.

When I knew Reese was about to arrive, I lit a few candles, put on soft music, and dimmed the lights. As usual, she knocked once before opening the door. One step in and she gasped. I stood in front of her with a single long-stemmed red rose in my hand.

"What's all this?" She looked around in awe. "Trent, there are so many flowers. When did you have time? And it smells so good in here."

"Lily made us lasagna."

"You do know it's not my birthday, right?"

"Yes, I know it's in August." I tapped my right temple. "After missing Valentine's Day, I have everything memorized up here."

"You mean in your phone's calendar?"

"Yeah, that too."

We both laughed, then her eyes went wide. "Wait, this is…" Her mouth shut and she frowned right before tears flowed from her eyes.

"Sweetheart, what's wrong?" Oh God, I screwed up. Did she hate this holiday? Was there a bad memory tied to it? Did some jerk hurt her? If that was the case, I'd find the loser and kick his ass.

Reese threw her arms around me. "Thank you so much, no one has ever done this for me before."

"Sweetheart, you haven't seen anything yet." I scooped her up and carried her toward the stairs.

"Wait, what about dinner?"

"We'll get to that. First, I want dessert."

She giggled and kissed my jaw. "Trent Archer, will you be my first valentine?"

"No, I'll be your last valentine."

"Even better."

EPILOGUE
Trent
OPENING DAY

I'D NEVER FELT SO NERVOUS in my life. It didn't matter that I had played in front of thousands of fans… millions if you counted television. Nothing could compare to the surge of adrenaline coursing through my veins. Not even the fact that our first game, as fate would have it, was against the Rockets.

Thankfully, we were up by three at halftime. We all walked into the locker room for the usual pep talk. I spoke to our starting quarterback, Omar Anton out of Dallas, who we drafted in the first round. Despite being a rookie, he handled the first half with the decorum of a veteran. I hoped that had been in part because of my coaching.

My phone chimed with a text I'd been expecting.

Kenzie: We're on our way.

She knew I wouldn't reply, but would also see that I read her text. Sending one back could possibly ruin everything. I gave the head coach a nod, he gave me a thumbs-up, and I raced out of the tunnel toward the field.

It felt so strange wearing black slacks, a golf shirt, and a pullover on a football field rather than a uniform. The cheerleaders danced a routine to a blaring country tune, some of the fans milled around, while other sat in their seats enjoying the break in the action.

When I stepped onto the turf, the crowd erupted in chants. It took a minute for me to understand they were saying my last name. The stadium vibrated with the combination of exuberant fans and the music. I acknowledged them with a wave of my hand and jogged toward the end zone. The last time I stepped foot on it with a crowd of people, was the day I met Reese... so to speak.

Back then the seats were mainly filled by Rockets fans. Today, I was happy to report, there were more of our fans filling the stadium. I'd been told by our account executive, our ticket sales had been better than ever before. Reese said it was because of me. Maybe there was a bit of truth to that, but the fact was, the Thunder had an amazing pre-season, and the fans were hyped.

I stepped across the goal line and looked up to

where she stood almost nine months ago. Wearing practically the exact same outfit and still looking sexy as hell, Reese stood and stared at me. I blew her a kiss and winked. She laughed, and Kenzie, my partner in crime, led her down the stairs to a waiting security guard, standing by the railing.

Reese leaned on the bar and yelled, "What are you doing?"

"Come here," I shouted back. She put her hand by her ear. Maybe this hadn't been such a great idea. Hustling toward her, I raised my arms. Understanding what I wanted, she climbed over, and I helped her down.

"What are you doing?"

Remaining silent, I laced my fingers with hers, and led her back to *my* spot, and dropped to one knee. Once again, the crowd's roar amplified. That was when I noticed the team lined up behind me. Not only the Thunder, but the Rockets were also there. Jackson stepped forward and waved his arms, quieting the crowd.

I flicked on my mic pack, and looked into her eyes. "Reese Parker, the day I met you, I was standing right here. I blew you a kiss and you gave me the finger." She laughed with tears in her eyes. The fans also found it funny as their chuckles rang out. "I think I fell in love with you that day and more every day since. You, Reese Parker, are the smartest, strongest, and most loyal person I know. Nothing in this world would make me happier than you agreeing to be my wife. So, Reese Parker" — I reached into my pocket and presented her with a three-carat diamond ring between my thumb and forefinger — "what do you say? Will you be mine forever?"

She bent down, not paying the ring any attention, and kissed me. The crowd flipped out, the reporters who had gathered took pictures. My family, who came for the game, stood behind Reese.

"Yes, Trent, I will marry you." Then she lifted her hand and extended her ring finger. Everyone around us laughed as I slid the platinum band on.

I kissed her until the ref blew his whistle. "I need to get back to work."

"You're crazy, do you know that?"

"Yeah, crazy in love with you. I told you, one day we'd replace that meme."

She glanced around at all the camera lenses pointed at us. "Yes, you did. Now go win so we can celebrate tonight."

"Babe, we've already won."

Read Jackson and Alexa's story in
Married to the Tight End
Coming May 17, 2022.
Pre-order today! Please visit
https://bit.ly/MarriedToTheTightEnd1

OTHER BOOKS *by* CARINA ROSE

Once Upon a Kiss
Once Upon a Dare
Once Upon a Duke
The Book Boyfriend

ABOUT the Author

Carina loves everything about romance. To her, it's the little things that matter. She also believes in insta-love, since she knew her husband was *the one* the first day she met him. She loves writing about swoony heroes and strong heroines. She adores that moment when a couple comes together and the hurdles they jump to get there.

When it comes to books, Carina loves to read all types of romance, but she seems to lean toward dark romance. She sometimes equates it to chocolate—sometimes you need a little dark to balance out the sweet. Whether enjoying dark or sweet romance, she reads to escape reality (even if it's for a few hours) and get lost in a fictional world. It helps her relax, and she hopes her books do the same for her readers.

Carina looks forward to sharing more love stories in her future novels.

CONTACT
Carina Rose

I love hearing from my readers. You all truly keep me going.

Please stay in touch!

Instagram: instagram.com/author_carinarose

BookBub: bookbub.com/authors/carina-rose

TikTok!: tiktok.com/@carinarosebooks?

Facebook Group:
facebook.com/authorcarinarose – Carina's Sweethearts

I also have a newsletter to help you stay up to date. I promise not to spam you. 😊

You can sign up here: bit.ly/CarinasNewsletter.

You can also reach me via my website carinarosebooks.com

or email me carinarosebooks@gmail.com

A NOTE FROM
the Author

Dear Reader,

Thank you so much for reading *Love in the End Zone*. It means so much to me. Those who know me know that I love football. These characters were so much fun to write. I hope you enjoyed reading about them as much as I enjoyed creating their story.

I also love hearing from you. Please don't be strangers. Feel free to drop me a note to let me know what you thought of *Love in the End Zone* or if you just want to hear about what I have going on. It's because of you that I get to do what I love.

Book reviews mean so much to writers, and I treasure each of them. If you have time, I'd love an honest review from you.

Once again, thank you for reading and for taking a chance on this book.

All my best,
Carina

ACKNOWLEDGMENTS

First, I'd like to thank my family for putting up with my long hours. I truly could not do this without your support. I love you all with everything that I am.

To my critique partner, Ann Marie Madden, thank you so much for being my sounding board and my shoulder to lean on! I am so appreciative of our friendship. I love you and am very grateful to have you in my life. You're more than a friend — you're family.

To my editors, Karen Lawson and Janet Hitchcock, from The Proof is in the Reading. I'm happy to be working with both of you. Thank you for taking care of my baby.

To MJ Fryer, LL Collins, and SE Hall, thank you for taking the time to beta read for me! Thank you for your honesty, comments, and suggestions. I'm so happy we all met through books and have become friends. I adore all of you.

Sommer Stein at Perfect Pear Creative. I don't even know what to say. LOL Except you have the patience of a saint. For everything we went through, I couldn't love this cover more. You're incredible. You always surpass my imagination. Thank you so much for all that you do. I appreciate you to the moon and back!

To Tami at Integrity Formatting. I couldn't do this without you! Thank you so much for making my books pretty! I appreciate you tons!

Thank you to Danielle Sanchez at Wildfire Marketing for your help in promoting *Love in the End Zone,* and for everything you do for me. I truly appreciate you.

To all the bloggers, thank you for the time you spend supporting authors and reading our stories. You take time out of your personal lives, and I am very thankful.

To the ladies in my reader group, Carina's Sweethearts, you are all wonderful. Thank you for joining me on this journey.

Most important, I'd like to thank the readers. We all love to read and talk about the books and characters we love, and I am so thankful for all of you. If you have time and would leave a review, I'd be very appreciative.

Thank you!

Xoxo

Printed in Great Britain
by Amazon